I0451930

LOSE YOURSELF
Get Lost in the Words

Anthology of Award-winning Short Stories

ISBN-10: 0-9851833-7-3
ISBN-13: 978-0-9851833-7-0

DEDICATION

This anthology is dedicated to those who
lose themselves—and enjoy it!

To the authors featured in this book: Scribes Valley thanks you for
your time, patience, trust, and talent.
.

CONTENTS

LOSING YOURSELF
A Foreword by David L. Repsher, editor

Get lost!

A simple phrase with complicated meanings. Taken one way, it can be considered quite rude and derogatory. Taken another way—the way this book intends—it is an extraordinarily great directive.

Writers desire to achieve that blissful sensation of being lost in the words, to find that the story has taken over and is writing itself, causing even the author to breathlessly wait to see what is going to happen next.

Readers also want that level of consciousness where their real world departs, and the words on the page transport them to places unknown.

The mere fact that you are reading this Foreword shows that you, too, are seeking to lose yourself in the written word, to leave everyday life behind, to be elsewhere.

You've come to the right place! The authors featured in this anthology have crafted remarkable stories with the capability and the power to take you out of this world. So, buckle up, turn the page, and:

GET LOST!

FIRST PLACE

THEM QUIET HOURS

"Do you see the head?" Esther pants, sweat dripping down her arms.

It's January, 1943. Her mother, Cora, sits beside her, occasionally dabbing Esther's forehead with a damp cloth. They are tucked away, Esther, her midwife Danetha, and her mother, in the pantry gutted by her father. Each new swell of pain makes Esther's legs shake, causing her face to burrow into her mother's side. At seven months, her mother could no longer stand the sight of her waddling around the house and confined her to a place where the neighbors could not see inside. Stopped most of their tongues from writhing in their mouths about Esther and whose baby she might be carrying. Her father removed the shelves to make room for a bed, lying on an iron frame just inches from the floor. Given to them by Lottie and Mr. Earley under the ruse that a family member was coming from out of town. Pieces of the statement were true which made it easier to tell.

Esther pulls strips of black paint from the bars by her head to distract from feeling Danetha's clawed finger prodding between her legs. Danetha peeks from underneath the sheet covering Esther's legs. The white scarf tied around her head glows against her dark skin, cheeks swelling as she wipes the sweat from her brow.

"Foolish child." Danetha's voice is anything but kind. "Your

9

baby done turned wrong. Need to flip right way round."

Esther's mother eases her back against the yellow-stained sheets draped over the mattress. A loose spring scrapes against the floor beneath her. Esther stares into her mother's almond eyes, feels the back of her hand caress the side of her cheek.

"I'm here," she says, bending over to wipe her lips on Esther's forehead.

Since her mother does not leave her side, Esther assumes the slap is meant to keep her awake. She takes her mind from the stinging sensation on her right cheek by noticing things around the room. Danetha's fat face dipping under the covers, meddling the baby that turned her stomach into a mountain, then had the nerve to get itself stuck. Her mother's twisted lip scowling down at her.

"Do it," her mother commands the midwife.

Esther shuts her eyes. She envisions some place better. Away from Danetha and her mother. She puts herself with Kazuo, remembering those quiet moments they shared when they could just "be" without looking over their shoulders. Her daddy always told her you learn the most about a person during them quiet hours spent together, but she never understood until Kazuo. Tasting the chocolate syrup from his lips, drowning in vanilla ice cream. His breath on her neck, between her breasts and along her thighs. Careful walks to the willow tree, cuddling under its leaves. Taking in the calm before he would dream up some kind of craziness about the house he would build for them, naming everything from cars to constellations.

And during those quiet hours spent together, she allows herself to love him.

Danetha clicks her tongue, her fingers prodding Esther's insides as she lets out a disgruntled moan. She might as well pull the baby out while she is fiddling in Esther's vagina.

"It's gonna hurt, Ms. Cora."

Esther's mother straightens, crosses her arms. She towers over

Danetha, her strong build overshadowing the delicate frame of the midwife.

"Will it hurt the baby?"

The darkness of the room hides her mother's face. Her voice should be softer, kinder, with a hint of concern. Esther repeats her mother's question in her head, struggling to pick a soothing, concerned or panicked tone to match.

"Won't know until it's out." A comment mixed with truth and delicately placed sorrow. It is apparent to Esther that Danetha has rehearsed this line before. She pats Esther's legs. "Stubborn. Like its mama."

Esther wishes she could kick Danetha in the face. Legs shaking, she is drowning in her sweat and whatever else is soaking the other end of the sheets. She wants the baby out, wants to hold the child against her chest and whisper the name of its father so it knows. Gazing into the child's eyes will allow her to dream again.

"Then do it." Her mother moves towards the corn silk curtains separating them from the kitchen. Esther reaches for her. A chill weaves through the spaces between her stretched fingers, her mother disappearing behind the curtain.

Danetha starts counting, head disappearing under the sheet. The front door slams. Esther's hand falls, fingers dragging against the wooden floors until she gets a splinter. Her mother must have forgotten something or gone to get help. She feels pressure, a gentle heat warming her stomach and rising to her chest. Her mother will come back. The pain is sudden, back arching but her eyes never leave the curtain. She screams, angry at herself for loving him. She screams at the baby to come out. She screams at Danetha to stop being so happy about everything. Esther decides to use both feet to kick her. Pain sends her hands flying behind her, grasping the iron bars of her bed. She will knock all of Danetha's teeth out, erasing that fake smile. Then, she will blacken her eyes so she can't use them. She screams loud enough for the world to hear her frustration.

Her fingers cling to the bars, chest rising and falling. She dreams of holding her baby, seeing the world swirling in its eyes. They will be hazel like hers. She will cradle it in her arms, kiss the top of its head and whisper Kazuo's name. She will teach it to despise Danetha, reveling no doubt in Esther's pain. Her child will know to be wary of the empty smile that masks the joy of torturing unsuspecting new mothers. *Mother.* Where was her mother? Cora had something she had to do. Something she must have forgot. Something important to pull her from Esther's side. Lips cracked, her eyelids shielding Esther from the world around her, beads of sweat slide from her pores. Where has her mother gone?

Month's ago, Esther had stared at her ceiling, listing all the places Kazuo might have gone. Five months into her pregnancy, she had stopped searching for him. She believed the nightmares and the burning in the back of her throat were temporary consequences for sleeping on her back instead of accepting what was growing inside of her body.

One night, something sharp had scratched her leg. She blamed it on a nightmare, tried to shift her leg. Something pulled it back into place. Her mother sat at the end of her bed, hands extended underneath Esther's nightgown. She rubbed Esther's swollen stomach. The baby kicked, sending erratic waves through Esther's outstretched skin.

"Mama," she yawned, rubbing the sleep from her eyes, "what are you doing?"

"Just checking." She squeezed Esther's foot. "Won't be long now."

The light in the hallway reflected off silver knitting needles her mother slid into the pocket of her pink robe. For weeks afterwards, Esther refused to let her mother near her, doing everything to make sure the baby was still kicking inside her.

Esther's head rises from the mattress. Her mother, hands moisturized with cocoa butter, pats her cheeks. *Is she back?* Two fingers stretch the skin around her eye. Dark curls escape from underneath a white scarf. Her mother hates white scarves. Claims they only attract dirt. Teeth reveal themselves, lips parting. No, not her mother. Danetha. Only she would smile like that, small teeth framed by her swollen lips. Something dries on Esther's cheek, hands turning her head from right to left. Esther spits in Danetha's face, disappointed by the dry air that passes between them.

"It's time to push." Danetha pinches Esther's lips together.

Esther pulls the sheet over her head. She hopes for a boy. She hears the front door open. A girl would come later. Her mother thrusts the curtains aside, an olive-green towel rolled and tucked under her arm. Esther's body tightens. A boy could survive in this world, Esther thinks. Her mother leans under the sheet. Hot breath tickles her feet. They would travel the world together. Her mother unwraps the towel. Esther and her baby, lost in a world of their creation.

With each push, Esther feels a part of her rising from the bed and flying all over California. To her father shoveling dirt, digging graves in the cemetery, keeping track of the war planes flying above, weaving stories about pilots, paintings of sky sharks and women wearing nothing but a handkerchief just coasting through the air to Esther and his grandchild as they sit on their tilted porch. Her father peeks in all the rooms until he discovers where her mother has moved her. He presses his ear against her stomach, listening, humming every song he knows. Tells all the stories he can remember, the ones his mother told him, the ones about the rabbits. When Esther was able to accept that Kazuo abandoned her, after burying his items in the graveyard, her father handed her his pants to mend.

She searched for a hole but all she found was a white piece of paper in one of the pockets. One side detailed the eviction of all persons of Japanese heritage. On the other, scrawled notes written by her father. Words interrupted by dashes, question marks without their dots. They translated to names, places and questions. Some had notes next to them. All were crossed out. No sign of Kazuo anywhere, like Esther dreamed up the year they spent together.

Now, Esther decides she wants a daughter. A girl will stay in her mother's arms until she is ready to challenge them. She will look like Esther but have Kazuo's innocence. She will memorize all the stories she hears from her grandfather, falling in love with the recurring rabbits. Esther will protect her. She will hold her until the time comes to release her. Her daughter will stumble, become confused and overwhelmed. She will learn to adapt. A girl will learn to adapt to this world.

One final push and Esther sees a small body, hands and legs fighting the air, passing between Danetha and Esther's mother. Esther leans forward, listens for a cry, coo or moan. She feels guilty for screaming at the baby. Danetha glances at her mother, tilting her head towards Esther. Esther fears the baby is deaf. She opens her arms, ready to receive her baby. Her mother sways. Esther grows anxious, ready to feel the warmth of the towel, pull back the flap covering the baby's face. Memorize every feature, no matter the gender. When she does not hear a cry, can no longer see the towel move in her mother's arms, Esther reaches out for it. She will put a finger under its nose, check to see if it's breathing. If not, she will give it her last breath.

"Mama?"

The baby cries. A small hand escapes from underneath the towel. Esther hates herself for smiling like Danetha. Why isn't she smiling now? Esther's arms begin to ache. The relief of hearing a baby cry after an extended amount of silence must be lost on Danetha.

"It's a boy," her mother finally says.

Esther giggles. "Let me see him."

Her mother bounces the baby in her arms. "Won't be long now."

"Mama?"

For the first time, her mother looks at her. Esther notices the wrinkles that line her forehead and cheeks. How gray her hair has turned. The tightening grip over the baby as her mother holds him closer to her chest. Her eyes shake in their sockets, glaring at Esther's spread legs and round belly. At Esther's face as her smile transforms into a scowl.

"Give me my baby."

"Everything will be okay," her mother says with a smile.

Esther leans into Danetha's arms, trying to understand what is happening. Her mother had stayed by her side the entire time. What changed? Even with her head in the toilet seat expelling everything inside her, her mother was always there rubbing her back. When she finished, her mother always offered her tea with honey to soothe her.

"Mama!"

Her mother shakes her head, stepping closer to the curtain.

Esther recalled the hours they spent sitting at the kitchen table, both sewing, her mother listening to her talk about the baby. Names, places he could sleep, what his favorite color would be. She would take him to the pond. Teach him how to climb trees, fish and swim. Esther would blush, joke that she would also need to learn how to swim. The baby and she would learn together.

And her mother would listen. She listened until she took the coffee can she kept hidden from Esther's father down from the shelf. She promised she would return, promising to take care of it. But the can returned full and Esther was banished to the pantry. If her mother could not stop the baby from coming, at least she could prevent all of Tombstone from seeing the child.

"At least let her see him!" Danetha pleads, cradling Esther's head in the crook of her arm.

Her mother lets the curtain fall past her face.

"Mama, please!"

Past the baby wrapped in the olive-green towel.

"Cora!"

Esther watches as Cora steps out into the cold January air, closing the front door behind her.

Esther cries, still reaching for her child. Danetha rocks her, rubbing her back and head before just holding her. Esther's mother always served her tea to soothe her. Tea with honey. Tea that burned the back of her throat. Tea that her father tasted. That made his eyes turn wild and a thick vein pulse on the side of his dark neck. Tea that made her sick for days and caused the baby to stop bouncing for a while. Tea that left a brown stain as the cup shattered against the wall. Tea that caused him to grab her mother, throw her on the couch. He would never hit her, but he let himself throw her when he needed to. That was one of those times.

Danetha wipes Esther's eyes with a white tissue from her pocket. The scent of lavender overwhelms her. The tissues Esther's mother gave her never smelled like this. They had a scent, one that made her nauseous.

"Wipe with these," her mother would say, passing Esther a pile of delicately folded tissues all smelling of soap.

The curtain settles. Danetha rests Esther on the mattress. A spring scrapes against the floor. Esther wonders if she hears Danetha whisper an apology or a prayer. Maybe both. Danetha wets a towel. Esther wants to kick her in the face. Something cool lies on top of her forehead. She imagines the sound Danetha's cheekbone would make as it shatters. The house is quiet. If Danetha tells her where her mother has taken her baby, she will spare her face, her fingers. She will convince her father to handle her mother. Esther places a hand on her hollow stomach. *Where has her baby gone?*

A chilled dampness presses against her cheek. When she opens her eyes, her father rinses his red bandanna in a wash bin resting on the side of her bed, white paint chipping away to reveal a rusted brown color underneath. Sore between her legs, pain still rolling in her stomach where her baby was being foolish, twisting and causing trouble, just hours before. Mind swimming with thoughts she cannot let loose. Dirt falls from the brim of his hat, dried mud cracking on the sides of his face. He pauses, dangling the bandana over her, small drops of water falling into the corners of her eyes.

Her father takes the corner of the cloth and presses the tip against her nose.

"Be still."

Her daddy must have carried her to her room, her favorite canary yellow robe with plaid patches sewed on the front to make pockets encases her sore body. Her walls a pale yellow, the windowpane splitting the moonlight into four streams of silver light, dust dancing as it ascends to the ceiling. Pieces of fabric cover the floor near her sewing machine, cotton bursting from the neck of a teddy bear as it rests under the needle. She hears the tapping of her father's toe against the floor, his shorter leg struggling to reach the surface.

"My—" her father presses the bandana against her mouth, water rushing down her dry throat. Her lips clench the surface, suckling any water the cloth is willing to give. Just breathing in gets the pain going again.

"Your mama," he admits, dipping the bandana in the bowl. He holds it over her, tilts his head up. Drops of water strike her face. She arches her neck, lets her mouth hang open as her father twists the bandana into a longer, outstretched spiral. "A meanness just sprouted in her."

"Daddy," as he lowers his arms, she places her hand on top of his, "he's mine."

Her father nods, dropping the bandana to the floor before placing his free hand on top of hers. "And he always gon' be yours."

Esther stares out the window, letting her father dab cold water on her face. He hums all the songs he knows, tells stories about the planes that flew over him while he was digging holes, whispers every name he can think of for a boy. Esther grins when he says *Floyd* to which he grunts, rubs his nose, suggests the name should sound a little more foreign given the boy's heritage. She repeats it, memorizing the way it sounds as it leaves her mouth, how her lips shape each letter, how her father drags the *o*.

The front door creaks. Her father kisses her hand.

She listens as his uneven footsteps carry him down the hall. A dim light glows, emphasizing the two shadows facing each other, the larger grabbing the smaller by the wrists. She turns away, her cheek nestling against the cool plush pillow. She presses her hand against her hollow stomach.

"Floyd."

Her parents yell down the hall. Her baby boy will survive. She hears glass shatter in the distance. She will travel the world and ask her father to join her. She hears her mother scream. All their stories will have rabbits. She feels the house shake.

Esther will abandon her mother. Travel the world and dream of Kazuo. She will venture out alone if she has to, her father unwilling to join her.

And she will adapt. A girl must learn to adapt in this world.

About the author:

K.B. Carle earned her BA from Old Dominion University in Virginia, MA from West Chester University in Pennsylvania, and MFA from Spalding University's Low-Residency program in Kentucky. "Them Quiet Hours" is a part of her novel-in-progress. When she is not exploring the realms of speculative, jazz, and historical fiction, K.B. avidly pursues misspelled words, botched plot lines, and rudimentary characters. Her work can be found in Pennyshorts, Sick Lit. Magazine, and Phindie.

SECOND PLACE

WEEZY'S GRANDMA
©2017 by Dorothy M. Place

Weezy came to visit her grandma, who lived in the dilapidated little house on the dirt road side of the bridge that spanned the creek running from the hill behind Kuglak's farm to Schoharie Creek. The bridge, old and wooden, connected the road in front of the house with the highway that led to town some eight miles away. It announced every arrival and departure of vehicles with the clatter of loose boards. Grandma English, as she was called by everyone, lived alone; that is until her younger son Clyde dropped off Weezy, his eight-year-old daughter, one day for a few hours but didn't return for several weeks.

Grandma English was a little woman, no bigger than a seventh grader and not much heavier than a grain sack filled with wet goose down. She had come to the place in her life where her hair was entirely grey and so wispy that it was hard to keep it tucked into the small bun that hugged the back of her head. The brown spots on her frail arms had long ago stopped multiplying and, as the years rolled by, folks swore she never looked a day older. Some said she was around seventy; others figured she was closer to ninety. Despite her frail body and many years, she took in Weezy with the same equanimity with which she sheltered the hens that strayed each summer from the city folks' house up on the hill, or any feral cat that sought warmth during the icy winter.

Weezy, on her part, took to Grandma English like every one of the stragglers that came to shelter in or around the little house. The regularity with which Weezy and her grandma lived was something the youngster hadn't known since her ma died: up earlier than the sun, off on the school bus by seven-thirty, dinner before dark, and back in bed at sunset. The orderly life gave such comfort to Weezy that she happily looked forward to every day. Her thin voice chirped through the house reminding Grandma English of the song sparrows mating call in early spring. It filled the old lady's heart with a fullness it hadn't possessed for many years.

"When's Clyde coming back?" Weezy had asked a week or so after she'd been left.

"Don't set right by me when you go about calling your pa by his first name."

Weezy was reading the book Clyde had bought for her just before he left her with his mother. It was about a small Chinese boy who lived on a houseboat on the Li River. The teacher had read the story to the class the first month of school and, since Weezy first heard it, she had pestered Clyde to buy the book for her.

She placed one finger on the sentence she had been reading and looked up twisting her long blondish hair into a tight curl with the fingers on her other hand. "That's the way he wants it," she said. "Clyde likes the ladies to think that I'm his little sister that come on late in his momma's life and got left orphaned early."

Grandma English watched Weezy's pale blue eyes fold into a tight squint as she spoke. Lord, she looked so much like Clyde when he was a boy. As far as she could remember, both Weezy and her son showed a strong resemblance to Sanford, her husband. But he had passed on so long ago, she had trouble calling up his face.

She looked away, snorted, and went over to the wood stove, her slipper-shod feet shuffled across the rough floor boards. She shook down the dead ashes and shoveled them into the scuttle. "Well," she muttered, "seems like everybody here about knows I never had a girl-child, and that I ain't dead yet." She picked up several pieces of kindling and threw them into the firebox. "Got to fill the stove's reservoir so we can have hot water to wash up in tonight," she said, picking up a pail and heading toward the creek.

Weezy followed her grandmother onto the porch, watched her scoop up the water and struggle up the creek bank with a full pail. Her back was bent low and the water sloshed over the edge, soaking her apron, the front of her dress, and her thick cotton stockings that sagged around her knees and ankles. The wet spots on her dress revived some of its original color, making it look as though the faded fabric was springing back to life.

"Why are you fetching water from the creek?" Weezy called down to her.

"Pump's broke."

"What'll you do when winter comes and the creek freezes?"

"Same's last. Chip the ice and melt it on the stove. You come on over here now and help me tote this into the house."

Several weeks later, just when the chill of fall was beginning to creep into the last of Indian summer, Clyde returned with a bag of groceries on one arm and a young lady on his other. Weezy was at school and Grandma English was out in the city folks' lower field collecting milkweed pods for dinner. She heard the boards on the wooden bridge set up a storm. When she looked up she saw his faded blue Chevy that tilted toward the driver's side swing around and stop in front of her house, raising a cloud of dust and scattering the city folks' chickens that were roosting on the woodpile. By the time she came close, Clyde and his young lady had settled into the rocking chairs on the front porch.

As Grandma English walked up the steps, Clyde smashed his cigarette underfoot and stood. "Brought you and Weezy some groceries," he said, putting his arm across his mother's thin shoulders. She wobbled slightly from its weight, then wiggled out from under his embrace and placed the basin of milkweed pods on the porch railing. She tucked some loose strands of hair into her bun, bent over, and peered closely at Clyde's new girl.

"Who's this little puppy you're dragging around with you now?" She pointed her finger at the girl. "Why, it looks like she just come off suckling her ma's tit."

The girl giggled, reached out, and took hold of Grandma English's outstretched hand.

"This here's Ida, one of them Hansons from up around Fultonham," Clyde said. "Ida, say hello to Ma. Talk up now, she ain't been hearing like she used to."

Ida giggled again. "Pleased to meet ya, ma'am." She covered her bright red mouth with her other hand and lowered her eyes.

Grandma English turned her back on Ida, picked up the basin of milkweed pods, and hobbled into the house, favoring her sore hip and clucking like an old hen. Clyde and Ida could hear her cleaning out the milkweed silk and washing the pods. She hummed "The Old Rugged Cross" as she worked.

After a while Clyde followed his mother inside. "There's a side of bacon in here," he said as he emptied the groceries onto the table. "And a candy bar for Weezy. She been minding you good?"

Grandma English nodded. "Reach up there and get down that spider," she said, motioning toward the cast iron frying pan hanging on a hook over the stove. "She's doing 'bout good as can be expected." She cut a slice off the side of bacon, placed it in the pan and set it on the wood stove. "Them milkweed pods'll be tasting mighty fine after I fry them in this here bacon fat. You having something to eat?"

"I'd like to, Ma, but I got to go."

"Now?"

Clyde nodded. He shifted from one foot to the other, and scratched the back of his neck. The spider warmed, the grease crackled, and the sweet aroma of frying bacon filled the room.

"Weezy's gonna to be real sad if'n you don't wait 'til she gets back from school. She pesters me about you every day."

"I got to get down to Barber's Ranch before dark. I hear he's hiring field hands to pick the last of the summer's table corn. I want to be there before all the jobs are gone."

Grandma English turned the bacon. Globules of grease escaped the skillet, skated across the hot stovetop until they cooled, leaving shiny black spots on the cast iron. "Not like you to be in a hurry to get a job." She added the milkweed pods to the frying bacon and a cupful of hot water from the stove's reservoir.

Clyde waited for his mother to say something more about his getting a job. When she didn't, he continued. "I'm marrying that little gal setting out there on the porch, and I want some spending money to take her on a honeymoon to Albany. Maybe show her the capitol building and go on as far as the Hudson."

"Why she ain't much older than Weezy." Grandma English shook her head. "What's she gonna say about having a youngster for a mother?"

"Weezy'd rather have a sister than a ma," Clyde said. "Anyway, it's all been settled. I asked Ida and she wants to come with me." He played around with the groceries he brought, making a pyramid out of the canned goods. After a short silence, he began pacing.

"What you got yourself all worked up over?" Grandma English asked.

"I was thinking that Ida could stay here until the job gives out." He stopped pacing and took hold of his mother's arm. "I have to sleep in the car—to save money—you know how it is. Not right for Ida to be sleeping out with a bunch of hired men."

"That why you brought them groceries?"

"It'll be no more than a week."

Grandma English grunted. "Ain't even a week's groceries."

When Clyde left, Ida stood on the porch waving good-bye with a white handkerchief. "I'll be missing you something terrible," she called. Her voice was drowned out by bridge boards thundering under the wheels of Clyde's departing car.

Grandma English hobbled out of the house and, without saying anything to Ida, walked onto the city folks' lower field, searching the high grass for eggs their hens might have left behind. Her head was so full of misery that she didn't hear the school bus stop to let Weezy out.

Weezy bypassed the house and walked to where Grandma English was bending over and picking up a clutch of eggs. "Clyde leave that here?" she asked, pointing to the porch where Ida was sitting in one of the rocking chairs.

Grandma English nodded.

"What did he go and do that for?"

Grandma English shrugged. "Here, take these back to the house and put them in the bowl of water I set out." She handed Weezy the dish of eggs. "And throw out the ones that float minding not to break the shells."

"When's he coming back?"

"Go on now, do as I told you."

Weezy skipped back toward the house while Grandma English hobbled off toward the far end of the field. *That boy'll be the death of me yet.* As she walked, she parted the tall grass, looking for more eggs. *If it isn't one thing with him, it's another ever since he returned from that war in Korea. Never gives a body time to get over one of his stunts before he starts right on in with another.* She picked a bunch of tender dandelion leaves and pushed them into her apron pocket.

That night at dinner, Ida sat smiling and picking at her food. "I ain't very hungry," she said. "Even though Clyde and me ain't had nothing all day."

"Eat then and stop fussing with the food." Grandma English bent her head over her plate and mopped up some of the bacon grease with a slice of bread.

"How long you staying?" Weezy asked.

"Until Clyde comes back for me."

"When's that?"

"Soon's he can," Ida said. "Then we're gonna get married and he's taking me on a honeymoon to Albany."

Weezy got up and cleared the dishes, taking Ida's plate away without asking if she was finished.

The next morning, after Orrin Franchel had delivered his full milk cans to the stand on the highway side of the bridge and loaded up the empty ones onto his wagon, he stopped to pass some time with Grandma English. Weezy was inside getting ready for school and Ida was still in bed.

"Morning, Orrin," Grandma English said as she came out of the house. She looked up at the sky. "More'n likely rain today as not. I can feel it in my hip." She settled herself into one of the rocking chairs.

"Has that feeling to it. Bad for the haying. If it holds off until tomorrow, we might get it in." Orrin pushed his straw hat back on his head, and steadied the horses with a small *tching* sound.

"Come on in and set a spell," Grandma English said. "I'm frying up a rasher of that side of bacon Clyde brought by."

"Not this morning, thank you kindly. Trace Bellinger's coming over to help bring in the last of the hay. He should be showing up soon."

"What's got into him? Never knew him to be agreeable about helping around less'n there's something in it for him."

"He knows my corn's ripe today, hisn'll be ripe tomorrow. Just thought I'd drop by to tell you the city folks asked to use my plow next spring." As he spoke, he pointed to the house up on the hill with the willow whip he held in his hand.

"What are they fixing to do with a plow?"

"Says he's gonna plant a vegetable garden on this lower field."

Grandma English shaded her eyes with her hand, looked out over the lower field and thought about that for a few minutes. Plowing up the field meant she couldn't gather dandelion greens or milkweed pods, and that the hens would go off and lay their eggs somewhere else. "That sure sets me up with a dry well, don't it?" she said.

"I wouldn't worry much about it," Orrin said. "It's a long way off and, come spring, it may turn out like Bill's maple sugar idea."

"How's that?"

"He tapped the black walnut trees on the fence line thinking they were maples. Boiled the sap for days and wondered why he didn't get no sugar. He looked pretty foolish when I told him Bellinger was the only one with sugar maples worth tapping around here."

"City folks," Grandma English shook her head, rocked harder and giggled like a young girl. "Never can tell what they'll be thinking of next."

Orrin laughed and nodded.

"How they gonna pull the plow?" Grandma English asked. "Harness it up to that wild young'un of theirs?"

"Said he'll use that Jeep he bought last winter. Has what they call four-wheel drive. Yesterday, he showed me how it works."

"My, my. I hope to live long enough to see that." Grandma English shook her head at the thought of a Jeep pulling a plow. "Yes sir, I surely want to see that."

"Ruth's digging potatoes today. I'll send her down with a sack of them for you and Weezy." Orrin tipped his hat, pulled it firmly on his head so that his ears pointed forward, and clicked his tongue. The horses set off toward home. The empty milk cans in the back of the wagon set up a racket that sounded like the world was coming to an end.

After Orrin left, Grandma English thought about the potatoes that would be coming later that day. She'd save the bacon grease from this morning and use it to fry the potatoes for supper. Maybe open one of those cans of beans Clyde brought for a side dish. Mercy, she never knew where the next blessing was coming from, but somehow they just kept coming.

It was over three weeks before Clyde returned. And when he did, it was one of the Slater boys from Summit Corners that dropped him off at the house. Grandma English had been inside washing the elderberries she'd gathered from the Vandenburg property a mile or so down the dirt road and thinking about the wine her father used to make from them. She sure could use a bottle of that now. It'd ease her bone aches and make her nights easier.

When the Ford truck stopped in front of the house, Grandma English recognized the popping sound it always made just before the motor died. She went out on the porch to see what Harlan Slater had to say for himself. His arm hung out the window and, when he turned toward her, he had that sly, hang-dog grin of his, like something was wrong but it wasn't his fault. He waved. "Morning, ma'am. Look what I brung home." He pointed his thumb in the direction of the passenger seat.

Grandma English knew what he had brought home without looking. "Bring him on in. I'll get some coffee ready." She disappeared inside the house and put the pot on the stove. "Weezy," she called up the stairwell, "your pa's finally come."

Harlan got Clyde as far as the front porch and pushed him into one of the rocking chairs. "Your ma's fixin some coffee," Grandma English heard him say. "You'll be feeling better after you get some of that into you." He stuck his head inside the door. "Got to be going," he called.

Grandma English went to the door. "What trouble you fixing to get into now?" she asked Harlan.

He laughed as he headed for the truck. The Ford's engine turned over several times before it caught. Harlan called out the window to Clyde. "I'll come by for you tomorrow. Get yourself looking pretty by then."

Clyde's head was sunk into his chest and he was slumped over in the chair. He didn't raise it when his mother sat next to him. She sat in silence, glad that Harlan had left. She had little use for him since he married her older son's daughter, Faith, and fathered seven children in just as many years. He spent most of that time loafing at Kenny's used equipment shop in West Fulton, bragging about what a gilt-edged life he's led since marrying Faith and having the children.

"Those young'uns are gold," he'd brag to anyone who'd listen. "All I gotta do is keep Faith producing, and the government money comes in."

Weezy came out on the porch. "Clyde," she said, "you're here."

Her father raised his head and gave her a weak smile, then turned to his mother. "That coffee ready yet?"

"You ain't looking so good," Weezy said.

"I ain't feeling so good."

"How'd your face get all cut up like that?"

Grandma English returned to the porch and handed him the coffee. He smelled like alcohol, cigarettes, and unwashed clothing. "Sure got yourself in a mess of troubles this time, didn't you?"

He raised the cup and sank his nose into it. His hands were shaking so he had to brace it against his lips to keep it steady.

"Where've you been?" Weezy asked. "We've been expecting you to show up for more than a week."

He brushed her words away with his hand.

"Answer the child," Grandma English said. "After being gone so long, you right enough owe her that."

"Ain't no use in asking because there's no way I can remember much of it." He closed his eyes.

"Where's the car?" Weezy asked.

"Sold for scrap."

"Sold it?"

"Weren't nothing left after the accident."

"Accident?" Weezy's pale little face became almost translucent and tears filled her bright blue eyes. "You mean we got no car?"

"Weezy," Grandma English said, "better be getting your breakfast. Willie will be here soon and you know he doesn't like any of the youngsters keeping the school bus on hold."

She gave her father a disgusted look and went into the house. Poor girl, Grandma English thought. A father shouldn't be such a burden on a child. That's not how the Lord planned it.

Clyde was still on the porch when Grandma English went off with Clara to collect black walnuts. Clara was never one to speak, at least not since she was little, but that didn't worry Grandma English none. She was accustomed to quiet. Besides, her neighbor from down the dirt road was a good one for helping her through the barbed wire fencing and filling the sacks. They worked silently,

28

collecting all the nuts from the ground and reaching up for the ones on the low hanging branches, enjoying the early autumn sun and each other's company. It was around noon when Grandma English, dragging a full burlap bag behind, got back to the house.

Clyde was still on the porch and Ida was sitting next to him. She had on her square-dancing dress with petticoats that hung below its hemline and socks that had a lacy fringe around the cuffs. Her white handkerchief was tear-wet and streaked with face powder and lipstick. She was sitting on the edge of the rocker, her one hand holding the handkerchief to her eyes and the other massaging Clyde's back. He was bent forward, his hands covering his face.

"But you said you were going to get a job picking the last of the table corn," Ida was saying.

"That's so," Clyde mumbled through his hands. He squirmed, as if trying to shake her hand off.

"If you been working all this time, you must've got some money."

Clyde didn't answer.

"You're saying there's no money?"

Clyde nodded.

"Where'd it all go? And where's the car?" Ida stood and stamped her foot. "You promised me a wedding and was gonna take me on a honeymoon."

Grandma English passed them and went into the house. The sound of a hammer pounding off the outer husk of the black walnuts covered Ida's wailing. She had seen this before; she regretted having to live it again.

The next morning, Harlan arrived around eleven. Grandma English was out back spreading the black walnuts in the sun to dry so they wouldn't mildew before she got around to cracking them and taking out the meat. She heard Harlan call into the house, "Clyde, you around?" She came back into the kitchen just as Clyde went out on the porch.

"How's she taking it?" Harlan was asking Clyde.

"Not going to set well with her."

"You mean you haven't said nothing yet?"

Ida came down the stairs and into the kitchen where Grandma English was sifting flour into a bowl. Ida's uncombed hair and puffy eyes made her look like a little girl who was recovering from a wupping. She sat at the table and watched while Grandma English stirred up the biscuit batter.

"Don't look like you got a powerful lot of sleep last night," Grandma English said.

Ida shook her head.

"Coffee's made. Want some?"

Ida nodded. "Clyde's money is all gone. So's his car. What's gonna happen now?" she asked.

"Seems like you better be talking to him 'stead of me." Grandma English poured a cup of coffee and pushed it toward Ida. "Might want to see what them two are talking about." Grandma English pointed to the porch with the rolling pin, then began to roll out the biscuit dough. If she spread it thin, there'd be some extra in case Harlan stayed on for breakfast.

The men fell silent when Ida came out onto the porch. Grandma English followed her with coffee for the men. The late morning sun had burned off the last of the mist, and a cottontail scurried out of tall grass and disappeared into the blackberry bushes. Grandma English watched some redwing blackbirds land among the tall reeds that grew on the highway side of the creek. It was about as nice a day as you could want except for the storm brewing on the front porch. Weezy came out in her pajamas and sat on the steps.

"What's gonna happen now, Clyde?" Weezy asked.

"You, me and Harlan's taking Ida back to her folks in Fultonham."

Ida screamed. "I ain't going back."

"Ida, honey," Clyde wheedled. Overnight his left eye had turned purple and scabs were beginning to harden the cuts on his face. "There ain't nothing left for me to do but to take you back to where you come from."

"But I can't go back. What with my pa all mad at us for you coming and taking me away and now me having a baby."

"Nice going," Harlan said. He snickered and leaned over, punching Clyde's shoulder with his fist. "Looking for some of that easy government money?"

Grandma English smacked her knees with her two hands. That boy never did pay no mind to what he was doing. She went into the house to check on her morning's baking. All this carrying on was going to make everyone hungry. She took the baking pan from the oven and sifted a light cover of flour over the golden-brown biscuits. Weezy came stomping into the kitchen.

"What's got you all wrought up?"

"Clyde says to pack. He's taking me away."

Grandma English looked at Weezy's pale blue eyes. They were all fired up from holding back tears. She nodded and turned away, placing the biscuits onto a white plate with brown cracks running every which way through the glaze. Neither spoke. The only sound was the creek rushing by and Ida's occasional sniffing.

After breakfast, Ida, looking pale as death, and Weezy, angry as a child can get, climbed into the bed of Harlan's truck and sat next to his dog, their backs pressed against the cab. Harlan whistled as he revved the engine and waited. Clyde came out of the house carrying Weezy's things in a cardboard box. He put his arm around his mother's shoulders and squeezed. She staggered a little under the pressure. Without saying anything, he walked around to the passenger side and climbed in.

Before the noise of the bridge boards gave way to the bird talk and insect trills, Grandma English was making her way to Tingue's apple orchard to pick up the fallen fruit. She'd bring back as many as she could carry and dry them for winter. She'd boil them up with some walnuts, a little sugar and, if she could get Mary Hilts to buy some in town, cinnamon. That'd make a fine breakfast when winter came on strong and the weather turned too cold to go out. She crossed the bridge and headed down the highway toward

Tingue's, glad for the sun's warmth on her tired bones. But where the fullness in her heart had recently taken hold, there was a small ache.

About the author:

Dorothy M. Place lives and works in Davis, California. Since submitting her first short story in 2008, she has had eleven stories accepted for publication in literary journals; three have been awarded prizes and one, a fellowship. Her debut, literary fiction novel, *The Heart to Kill*, has been published by SFA Press (2016). A collection of fifteen short stories has been compiled and being prepared for marketing this spring. Her second novel, "The Search for Yetta," is in process.

THIRD PLACE

NOTHING TO WRITE HOME ABOUT
©2017 by Colin Brezicki

How ludicrous to get worked up over a postage stamp. It was such a little thing. Didn't people actually say something was *no larger than a postage stamp* to show how tiny it was?

And what had Matt said to her the last time he came home? *Life's way too short to sweat the nickels and dimes, Mum.*

But he didn't understand. She and Matt were like chalk and cheese. He, free-spirited and unbothered, while she fretted over the minutiae—a forgotten birthday, an overdue hydro bill, a missed garbage pickup—never mind nickels and dimes, she was chafing over the pennies this time, letting a postage stamp get under her skin.

And right at a time when she was actually doing something to be different and break with the past. Here she was, driving alone on the left side of a very narrow road in a rented car and heading for the remotest part of a country she hardly knew. Cape Wrath on a whim. She didn't do whims, but she was doing this and not altogether sure why.

What was she thinking? Dumping her coach tour at the hotel, hiring a car and racing up the west coast of Scotland so she could stand on a cliff edge and look out to sea? She hoped there would be more to it than that. Cape Wrath was secluded, wild, and best of all, unpopulated. And there was little thinking involved. It was sheer impulse. An urge to cut loose, to break the surface and gulp in air. To be for once in her life intrepid, or as Matt would say, *radical*.

So why had she brought along the postcard? Why could she not have been intrepid and radical enough to leave it at the hotel for a day, and then tomorrow go out and buy a stamp that fit?

You obsess about things, Mother. Sometimes you just have to let go. Liz was right, like her brother, and both adding that her anxiety had worsened with age.

She should have started the address further down the card; but she had bought the stamp first, so how could she know it would mask her daughter's name and all of the address except for the province and country? If she had thought about it she would have affixed the stamp before writing the card. That's the way her father would have done it.

Such a ridiculously large stamp, even one to mark the Queen's ninetieth birthday. An archived photo of Her Majesty wearing a lemon coat and matching sponge cake hat, not quite smiling and sitting in an open car beside Nelson Mandela, he waving to the crowd and happy as Larry.

It was lovely as stamps went, but this one wasn't going anywhere. Not on that postcard.

She'd hoped to find a post office on the way north, but so far all she had seen on the convoluted road from Ullapool were highland cattle and sheep, some isolated hill farms, and a gas station without a convenience store. There would be no post office at Cape Wrath. There was nothing at Cape Wrath, and that, she reminded herself, was the point of her journey.

She could make it there and back before dark, the man at the car hire assured her, especially with the long daylight hours this far north. She had informed Angelika, the tour chaperone, that she would check in with her when she got back to the hotel. It was all she could do, having decided against bringing her cell phone on holiday. Angelika was surprised, as well she might be. "It's a terrible road, Grace, all twists and turns, and there's nothing to see at Cape Wrath. Why would you want to go there?"

"I like the name." It made her think of winter storms pounding the coastline. She omitted to tell Angelika that she would scream if she didn't get away from Myra Gladstone and the group for one day at least.

Gems of the Highlands were heading off that morning for John O'Groats—a tacky little outpost, someone said, that didn't top her list of places to see despite its claim to be at the top of the country. On their way back the group were to visit the castle at Mey, but that didn't appeal either. It was too soon after Urquhart for her to tour another castle, especially an inhabited one like Mey where she would feel like an intruder. She always hung back when the group poked about inside a castle that was still someone's home. After Clayton died and she put the house up for sale she resented open days when she had to vacate her home so strangers could traipse through the rooms and gawp at the furnishings and family photos.

But there were no castle stops on this road and less likelihood now of a post office. She felt anxious again.

The card had to arrive home before she did. To show up ahead of one's postcard was slipshod and negligent. Life was all about shipshape and Bristol fashion, as her dear father used to say. *A place for everything, Gracie, and everything in its place.* Due dates observed, postcards stamped before addressing, and mailed in time.

Writing another card and leaving room for Her Majesty's birthday stamp was also out of the question. The postcard she had selected in the gift shop at Urquhart Castle was perfect—a striking photo of the ruins etched against the deep blue of Loch Ness under a moonstone sky. She wanted Liz and Ken to imagine her touring the castles of Scotland in perfect weather and being immensely grateful for their retirement gift, even if it wasn't her choice.

Coach tours, even cruises, were never on her so-called *bucket list*, and she was surprised that Liz had booked it before asking. Yes, she always wanted to visit Scotland—her father had often told her stories about his childhood in Edinburgh—but she intended to go by herself one day and not bother much with castles.

But Urquhart was such a surprise—easily the highlight of her trip so far—and that's what made the postcard special.

It had stirred something. For starters, the weather was nothing like the sun-washed picture on the card. She had stood on the mound above the castle ruins and watched a magnificent storm move up the loch. Its vaporous sleeves hung like a weeping cypress, obscuring the hills and darkening the waters as it approached.

The rest of the group escaped inside the visitors' centre the moment they felt the first fat drops; but Grace zipped up her anorak, yanked the hood over her head and made her way down the slope to the castle. A heavy mist already shrouded the ruins, lending them a melancholy aspect that comforted her as she picked her way along the broken walls. It was exhilarating to be on her own in the rain while the rest of the group sat inside the visitors' centre sipping their *cappuccinos* and grumbling about the weather. Out in the storm she didn't feel alone anymore. This was real. She bought the postcard before getting back onto the bus.

On the way out of the parking lot, Myra Gladstone remarked in a loud voice, "There you were, Grace, in all your glory—like a drowned rat. Did no one ever tell you to come in out of the rain?" And then she looked around to see that the others were smiling too.

They were a mirthless, disagreeable lot, mostly. The way they competed over their grandchildren—little prodigies of course, every last one—and their own ever so busy social lives, the charities they quilted, biked and baked for now they were retired.

How did we ever find time to work? Ha ha.

Out would come the smartphones, with much stroking and tapping to display photos of splendid homes and perfect families; but the proud smiles tightened a little when it was someone else's turn.

The husbands stared out the windows, mostly, or nodded off in their seats. She wondered if men just became more subdued after they retired or if a coach tour of Scottish castles wasn't their cup of tea either. It would never have appealed to Clayton, even a high-end tour that offered business class from Pearson International, five star hotels and gourmet meals, a bus like a motor home with its bar, tinted panoramic windows, reclining plush seats, lounge music and a separate gents' and ladies' at the rear.

Myra Gladstone had been quick to establish herself as the group's mother hen during the meet-and-greet in the VIP lounge at the airport. Grace imagined her as a schoolgirl, haranguing the meek and the uncertain, making life miserable for anyone who resisted her importunities. Her husband, a tall, well-tailored man with a sweep of white hair and a rueful look, had been something in hedge funds. Myra assured everyone they had done very well thank you.

Normally, Grace sat with Maria Di Franco, because they both liked to gaze in silence at the still lochs and the hills yellowed bright with gorse.

Among competitive and aggressive people like Myra Gladstone, Grace made herself disappear, though not as dramatically as she had done this morning.

Has anyone seen Grace since breakfast? Maria Di Franco would ask, and Angelika the guide would inform them. Maria would miss her, and have to sit alone on the long ride to John O'Groats, which was regrettable of course; but Grace had learned long ago that everything comes at a cost.

Making herself invisible was a skill she acquired during her drawn-out marriage to Clayton. Invisible but not idle. Never that. Something else she owed her father. *Idleness is the devil's workshop, my wee Gracie.*

She had done the lion's share of raising Elizabeth and Matthew, while working her way up to academic archivist at the McLuhan Library. Clayton did what he regarded as his bit in paying the hefty school fees. He earned an exorbitant salary flying first class across the continent, selling his technology, riding high on expenses and back-slapping camaraderie wherever he went—sales conferences, executive retreats, marketing summits. He cut a dashing figure with his expensive suits and easy charm, but in those hand-made leather shoes he could run roughshod over his rivals, and his family too, especially poor Matthew who seemed destined to disappoint his father no matter what he did.

Clayton wasn't much impressed by what she did either—no six-figure salary for a start—and one day he announced that her shelf life had expired. She thought he might be leaving the marriage, but he meant libraries, *shelf life* being his idea of a joke.

"I don't like to say it, Grace, but books are done. It's screen now. Internet not archives. You'll have to upgrade or be left behind."

No kidding. Six weeks later the Board of Governors blind-sided her in approving a complete makeover for the McLuhan Library—bookshelves replaced by a user-friendly space with computer hubs and wide screens, and a student café where lattés trumped silence as the order of the day.

"What'd I tell you, Hon? You've got yourself stuck in the past."

"My husband lacks grace," she muttered to herself, and then smiled at what she had said. But in the end, it was *his* demise—the irony of which she tried not to dwell on—that funded her early retirement and allowed her to walk away from a library without books.

She thought again of her solitary jaunt in the downpour at Urquhart. And now this wild, sudden charge up the coast. Such impulsive, even reckless, behaviour, and so out of character. Mostly.

Mum, be sure to send us a card, okay?

It wasn't that she'd written anything important; one never said much in a postcard. It was the sending that mattered. Letting people know they were in one's thoughts.

Having a lovely time with a very nice group. Three days in Edinburgh and I found Spottiswood Road where Granddad grew up. Silly me, I had a little cry when I saw the house. Shopping on the Royal Mile, and a military tattoo at the Castle. Stirling and Oban after that and now Ullapool. John O'Groats and Castle Mey tomorrow. Hurray! Castles everywhere! Weather iffy at times but overall amazing, just like Urquhart in the pic. Forever grateful to you both. Really. Love to you both and a special hug for Arn and Bub.

Gram.

What names they all had. Stripped down to monosyllables, as Liz and Matt had done. Apt, really, with everyone too rushed to spell things out anymore. Those impossible ciphers in Liz's text messages—sentence parts lopped off worse than a postcard or a telegram. Okay, maybe not worse than a telegram. But at least a telegram had something important to say. Anyway, names had abbreviated with the times. Matt. Liz. Ken. Arn. Bub.

Bub isn't short for anything, Mum. We just like the name.

At least *Grace* could only ever be *Grace*, her father's choice. Irreducible and invisible Grace.

But now she was *Gram* as well, and she wasn't comfortable with that.

She didn't know how to behave as *Gram* because little Arn and Bub always seemed keen for her to be gone almost the minute she arrived so they could get back to their devices. They had long lost interest in the stories she read to them and, yes, that was natural at their age, but even when she asked them to show her the games on their screens they grew impatient. Their behaviour did little to help her think of herself as *Gram*. The thought did occur—and now she wished it hadn't—that they were glad their parents had arranged for her to go away.

You'll have a fabulous time, Mum. You'll meet lovely new people. And you had such a rough time before Dad died.

That was true enough. And after as well. The sharp guilt rose now like reflux. She had wished *him* away in the end. Yes, she had, and there was no denying it. But really, a month on life-support? What was the point of that? Every day she spent holding his damp, spongy hand, staring at the blips on the monitors and pretending he even knew she was there, was another day added to his life and subtracted from hers.

And so, the evening came when she spoke those terrible words—more to herself than to his comatose form, but still. "Do you suppose you might just let go now? Don't you think you'd be better off?"

And the shock when an hour later he died. Flat-lined just like that. The doctors had their own explanation, but he had heard her, she knew. Somewhere inside that diseased and bloated body, once so lean and strong, like on the day he climbed the bleachers at a Golden Gaels homecoming and asked her out—on a bet, he told her after they were married, but never mind—he heard her say he should let go. And for once he obliged her.

Matt took it harder than Liz, surprisingly. He never seemed to miss his father when he was away on business, and he kept his distance when Clayton was home again. Matt left the summer he graduated and came back just once during his father's illness. And yet at the memorial he was so distraught, almost inconsolable. All so unexpected. Then he was gone again.

He was in Israel now, or maybe it was Jordan—a dangerous country, regardless—riding his Vespa and living off what work he could find. He came home every couple of years when Grace sent him the fare and an ultimatum. But after a week or two he would grow restless and then head back to wherever he had parked his scooter.

She would always love her aimless, wandering Matthew, but more and more she missed him in an odd way, maybe less like a son now and more like a phantom limb.

He didn't send postcards from wherever he happened to be: Morocco, Turkey, Algeria—did these places even *have* postcards? she wondered—and so he never stressed out over a stamp. Never sweated the nickels and dimes. But he texted every now and then to tell her he was okay, puttering around a country whose location she sometimes had to look up.

"Did you never wish to come home and stay? Get a job and settle?" she asked him last Christmas.

"Wherever I am *is* home, Mum. That's how it is for me." He

made it all sound simple. Home is where you are. Same for mollusks, she thought. Or were they gastropods? Creatures that carried their homes around with them. Better sounding than itinerants or vagrants either way.

Matt made her think of how the very first cameras worked. They could photograph only stationary objects—trees or buildings, say—because imaging took several hours. And so, if a person walked through the scene during exposure time they would leave no impression. That was Matt. Invisible. Like *Kilroy was here.*

Like her too.

The thought came unprompted and unsettled her. For all her family and career and acquisitions, what impact had she made, having spent sixty years being invisible? And what was she doing right now? Heading for the remotest point in the Kingdom in search of—what—a postage stamp?

She parked at the jetty and joined the tiny group already waiting for the ferry. She could see it, not much bigger than an outboard, coming toward them from the opposite shore where a minibus waited to take them out to the headland.

She paid the ferryman, a laconic old salt, and took a seat in the stern.

Her group included a blond Nordic-looking couple, he with ice-blue eyes and perfect teeth, she with a tattoo of musical notes trickling down the side of her neck. A paunchy fellow in a baseball cap sat beside a possum-faced woman who kept eyeing the high water around the boat. A thin, elderly man with a trim white beard and narrow eyes sat in the bow and stared back at the jetty like he was having second thoughts.

No one attempted to converse over the wail of the engine. She watched the gulls wheel above the boat as it troughed the water.

On the bone-shaking minibus ride across the moor, Eric, their driver, delivered his spiel about Cape Wrath. *Most remote part of the British mainland—army artillery site—"But not today, you'll be glad to hear!"—spectacular views of the lighthouse and the great beyond—"Wrath" derived from the Norse meaning turning place—Viking ships turned at the headland and made for home.*

A turning place—so nothing at all to do with storms pounding the coast, though she was sure they did.

An hour's ride on the pitted, broken road took them to the very rim of the world: a couple of outbuildings, the lighthouse and the abyss beyond.

She separated from the others and, leaning into the gusts, climbed the grassy slope to the cliff edge. Turning her face to the sea, she raised a hand to shield her eyes against the wind. It tugged at her lashes and roared in her ears. Above the rush, she heard the *clink clink* of the rope ties banging against the metal flagpole and looked up to see the blue and white Saltire snapping in the wind. The whitewashed tower brightened whenever the sun broke through. Far below her, the gulls cried and rose on the crosswinds that swept in from the sea.

Eric had taken the others inside the canteen *for a tea and a wee*. The minibus stood empty, rocking slightly in the gusts.

To the north, she could see the undulations of Orkney, suspended between sea and sky, and to the east, Dunnet Head, a dark leviathan brooding on the grey water. She would like to have taken some photos but in her hurry to get away that morning she had left her camera at the hotel.

She stood for a time thinking nothing—her mind empty—and then turned to look back across the moor at the world she had come from. To her right was the family. Her daughter's family—and now she couldn't remember their names. How absurd was that? *Liz*, of course. And Ken. The boys, Arn and Bud.

Looking to her left she imagined where Israel might be—or was it Jordan—and Matt riding his Vespa, alone or maybe with a friend. For a time, she had wondered about his sexual persuasion, but none of that mattered now. She hoped he had a friend.

The party emerged chattering from the canteen and walked up the rise to where she stood. Then everyone was silent for a time, gazing out to sea and surrendering to the emptiness.

Eventually, the phones came out and selfies were taken against the lighthouse and the horizon beyond. Baseball cap and possum lady posed solemnly, his phone held out on a stick like he was toasting a marshmallow. The Nordic couple laughed when they saw their photo. The elderly man aimed his camera at Dunnet Head, now luminous in the bright sun.

Stepping to one side, she opened her purse and took out the postcard. She stared at it for a moment. Then she unfolded her wallet and found the stamp. She peeled it away from its backing and placed it over the address. Slowly raising her arm, she held the card up to the wind.

When she let go, it hung for an instant as if uncertain what to do. Then a gust snatched it and swept it up into the glare. Mailed at last.

She smiled.

The possum lady looked away.

Eric announced a photo op before the drive back to the ferry. Grace stood in the middle of the group, between the girl with the musical tattoo and the elderly man, who took her arm like it was something he was expected to do. His grey eyes twinkled for a moment and he smiled for the picture.

Everyone gave Eric their email address so he could send them the photo.

It would remind her of the day she stood at the beginning of everything that was to come.

On the ride back in the minibus, half-listening to Eric talk about myths of the Orkneys, she thought she heard him mention *selfies* and wondered what on earth cell phones had to do with ancient folklore. But when he elaborated on the magical seals that once came ashore to be transformed into young women, she realized he had said *selkies*.

Staring out at the moorland she felt her heart race with a new excitement she couldn't begin to explain.

She would send her Cape Wrath photo to Matt when she got back to the hotel.

About the author:

A retired English teacher (surprise!) Colin Brezicki has written three novels and a collection of short stories. The novels remain unpublished, while some of his stories have won awards in Canada, New Mexico and New York. His feature articles have appeared in *The Globe and Mail* and in education journals in Canada and the U.S. Any writing ability he has was acquired by reading fiction writers more skilled than he could ever hope to be. Daughter Catherine's sharp editorial eye has also proved indispensable. He lives in Niagara-on-the-Lake, Canada

THE FIRE NEXT DOOR
©2017 by Lisa Ann Battalia

Betsy Carter's screen door slaps shut. It almost catches her backside as she pushes through it and steps onto the patio carrying a tray filled with pink glasses and a swirly-glass pitcher. In Betsy's backyard, summer-time props are lined up at attention—citronella lanterns, a drink tub filled with ice and soda, extra wood stacked by their new fire pit.

Laura Tucker sees this all from her bedroom window next door, looking down, helpless to salvage a beautiful summer evening. If it weren't for the smoke, and the party noise that was soon to crescendo from the Carter's backyard, Laura would have turned off her air conditioning and opened the window. Let in the lovely breeze, grateful for the opportunity to chase away the summer-stale air that has collected inside.

Instead she turns from the window and looks at her hands, fingers spread of their own volition. She stares at them unseeing, trying hard to remember why she came upstairs in the first place. Things are seeping from her, her short-term memory and attention to detail. If she could just pull her fingers together. It's funny how clearly she can recall the details of a trip she and Mark took long ago, before the kids were born, before, even, they moved into this house. They had traveled to Alaska, to a hotel so remote that guests had to leave their cars behind where the dirt road ended at a swift moving river. In an old chairlift seat, pairs took turns pulling themselves over the water, hand over hand, on the cable above. She and Mark were the last to go. It was so easy to glide the chair to the middle of the cable, but they had struggled hard on the upswing and the other guests, in their excitement to get to the place they all were headed, failed to turn around and see that Mark and Laura could have used a little help. Now, left to dangle she can't even rely on Mark's stronger arms.

She looks back out the window. The Carters have set up a croquet set tonight. Honestly. Who plays croquet? She is not unaware that the Carters have become her private obsession. Not unlike the distraction of reality TV, she is observing someone else's mess, ignoring what might be termed her own. Ostensibly, she could be washing dishes, but just as often she is stuck in front of an entirely empty sink, wasted water running, because there is no one at home who needs tending to. Because it's Mark's weekend with the kids. In this way, she had watched as the Carter's fire pit project unfolded over the course of the spring like a bad recipe for family togetherness. There were weeks' worth of Betsy's saccharine entreaties to get everyone to pitch in.

"It will be so much fun when the fire pit is finished. S'mores any night of the week."

Then, in one weekend afternoon, Betsy's husband, Jack, made short work of it. He dug a hole in the ground and surrounded it with a short wall of bricks Soon after, the fanned wooden chairs arrived, each one a different bright color, as if to insist that any time spent around the fire pit would be fun, fun, fun.

Tonight, the gathering is small. Betsy's parents have joined them but have barely spoken a word, even to each other. They are seated at the patio table but appear only to have moved arms, at the elbows, to bring tall, sweating glasses to lips. Something strong Laura suspects—she has shared strong cocktails with Betsy's parents in summers past. Betsy hovers on the patio, and Laura finds herself pulling up her bedroom window—just an inch—and the air-conditioned hush of her bedroom is replaced by Betsy's voice, sweet, piercing.

"Mom, Dad, you've got to try these. It's a new recipe."

Betsy thrusts her kitschy swimming pool-shaped serving tray in her parents' direction, and her mother puts her hand up as if in self-defense. So, Betsy turns to Owen, her oldest child, college age now. But he turns his face away, looks up into the trees, where, following his gaze, Laura notices that the fireflies have begun their lovely evening light show.

Enough. She shuts the window. She heads downstairs and pulls an opened bottle of white wine from the refrigerator. Pours herself a large glass, grabs a section of the Sunday paper she's been trying to work her way through all week, and finds a spot in the family room. She picks a long article and slips into the cocooning embrace of the couch. August's pause will end soon enough, to be replaced by soccer side-lines and homework battles and, on alternating weekends, nights empty and cold enough to notice the decomposing. She brings her wine glass to her lips.

There is a sudden, loud sound. The screech of car tires so unexpected on their quiet street that Laura drops her glass. Her first thought is how best to blot the spill from the expensive carpet, but she stops herself and walks quickly to the front of the house and pulls parallel the slats to open the living room shutters. A car, presumably the one that made the awful sound, is parked in front of the Carter's house. Someone has already jumped out, a young man, Owen's age, maybe older. He is yelling something she cannot hear through her double pane windows. Still, she can tell that ugly words are being hurled like grenades at the Carter's house.

She pulls the shutter's cord, instinctively wanting to distance herself from such raw anger. She hated how aggressive Mark could be driving, jamming in and out of lanes, cutting off other cars and disparaging their drivers, his entire face turned into one big scowl. It makes her fear for kind things. Then she hears the peel of the tires as the car pulls away. She waits, shutters still shut, for something to happen. There should be follow up activity, police cruiser lights and sirens, neighbors rushing over, anxious about what happened and is everyone okay. But nothing happens and Laura knows she is not in a position to do the follow up, not these days.

She waits all the following day for an explanation. Maybe even an apology. Life next door, however, seems to return to normal. When the kitchen door periodically opens, Laura can hear Betsy. Her voice. The way she coos and swirls it, as if whipping cake frosting into fluffy peaks. Does she actually believe that if she is cheerful enough, her children will never be touched by life's bared teeth?

She and Betsy had been close. There was a time, near the beginning, when the two families were more than just neighbors with the same model of house and matching side doors that opened onto a shared driveway. Her two children were young then, both under four, and life seemed to spill through the side doors and onto the driveway. Laura had been grateful for that. Once she was outside, shifting weather or a simple wave from a neighbor out for exercise, could keep at bay the isolation that would overtake her, that surely would overtake any mother at home with young children, if she did not fling open her house each morning, and cast herself onto the world.

Owen, Betsy's oldest, was nearly eleven when Laura and her family moved in. Owen's sister was nine, their younger brother six. Owen and his sister could ride skateboards and two-wheel bikes. Her children stared, sudden saucer-round eyes filled with adoration. Perhaps that brought the Carter kids out more often. Chicken or egg? But the Carter kids seemed to fall in love with hers, even though they were hapless bundles of energy determined to get in the way. Laura spent hours on the periphery, with something to read, trying to be both hands off and available. She was traffic cop and "boo boo" kisser, and she watched the Carter kids frequently, as requested.

"Mrs. Tucker, look at me, no hands..." There was always some modest but new skill to be admired. The younger Carters liked so much to be watched that they usually forgot half-way through what they meant to show her, not that it mattered, so long as she turned vaguely in their direction. Owen was different. His tricks were more difficult and he asked her to look only after he had practiced and practiced. His skateboard required real skill not to fall off and break something. Owen would screw up his face in concentration, make sure she was really looking, and then work hard to finish well. He did not always succeed but Laura cheered regardless, glad that an ER trip had been averted. Owen, though, had his own strict criteria, and his face would blaze with disappointment. She wondered how he made it through a school day. Of course, there were the times when Owen had nailed it: the skateboard took flight and, as if with magic glue, stayed attached to his feet, and he landed still balanced on his board. His look was lovely then. As if he believed God had witnessed his accomplishment.

Betsy rarely came out. She did editing work from home and, Laura guessed, took advantage of the quiet inside her house. Eventually, Betsy must have noticed the kind, consistent attention Laura gave to Betsy's children. Or perhaps she noticed how often Laura was alone with her own kids when Mark worked late or was traveling. She began to ask Laura and the kids over occasionally, to join them for dinner on their back patio. Laura would bring something from her refrigerator. Sometimes, when Jack had also been away, she and Betsy were free to talk about the things that women talk about.

The Carter kids had gotten busier, though, as school-age kids do, with friends and sports and school activities. She and Mark socialized with younger families in the neighborhood. Dinner in the Carter's backyard happened less and was more formal, always with husbands and other guests, but Laura continued to enjoy her time with Owen. At the beginning of his teens by then, it had been impossible to imagine him surly and self-centered. Instead, he would tell her about his friends and things that happened at school and his worries about the world's scary problems. But when Betsy got wind of the conversation she would quickly shift to her strident, "happy" voice, still candy-coated, but not to be contradicted.

"Owen," she would say, "let Laura enjoy her evening." She would ask Owen to get something from the kitchen, then insert Laura into an adult conversation.

Laura glances over from her kitchen window. That damn croquet set! It's still set up. She can't quite believe that another backyard party is unfolding, after the car and the hurled insults from the angry kid. But food trays and drinks have been assembled, and there is the youngest Carter kid acting like a clown with his croquet stick. He is working hard to finagle his mother's laugh, a sound that makes Laura cringe. But Betsy doesn't, she's not paying attention to her youngest son, she is looking at Owen. In the late-early-evening-still-light of summer, Laura can see that Owen has lost weight and shaved off most of his thick, dark hair. Both exaggerate the hollows behind his eyes. He seems merely to be going through the motions of playing a round of croquet with his brother.

Is it becoming an issue how much time she spends watching her next-door neighbors? Mark returned the kids to her that afternoon. She'll take them to the neighborhood pool. They can eat dinner at the snack bar. She might even go swimming with them instead of remaining hidden and huddled on the pool deck in a lounge chair with a book. They can stay until the pool closes at ten. Her kids will think it an adventure, swimming that late at night. In the dark, anything imagined can be real. At least that still holds true for her daughter and her guilelessness will draw in her older brother. A crocodile may have escaped from the sewer system and made its way into their pool. Lurking. They will have to set a trap and catch it, staying in the water until the sky is as dark as a bruise.

On the drive home the kids are quiet in the back seat. They'd already washed the chlorine out of their hair. Her daughter changed into her pajamas in the dressing room. Only three traffic lights between pool and home but Laura still has time to think about how to get through the rest of the night. Her tuckered children will go straight to bed and fall asleep. She can sit in her most comfortable chair, select her playlist "For a Glass of Wine"— she'd named it in a long forgotten playful mood— and read until her eyes are tired.

She smells the acrid smoke and hears the stridency of a "pit" party the minute she turns into the driveway. Damn it. She and the kids have not stayed away long enough. She struggles to imagine a new plan for the evening. She can still tuck the kids in quickly, take a sleeping pill and bring her book to bed, pull down her window shade without even glancing in the Carter's direction. She slides open the van door and the kids stumble out.

Just then there is the distinctive, disturbing squeal of tires. A car is pulling up far onto the Carter's front yard. Her groggy kids turn instinctively in the direction of the sound. A young man—the same one as the other night Laura guesses—jumps out of the passenger side of the car with a hoody pulled up over his head. He grabs for something in his jacket pocket. Laura pushes her children down and squats. From that height, she can see through the van's windows that the young man is doing something to the Carter's lawn. She hears a hiss. It's a can of spray paint. What did she think it had been, a gun? He glances over and probably can see her through the window. She feels silly crouched down, as if in need of protection from a can of paint. So, she stands up and shoos the kids through the kitchen door, saying too loudly that it's late, and time to get to bed. Once inside, her kids want to run to the front window but she forbids it.

"Upstairs. Teeth brushed. Bed in thirty seconds," she barks.

Only after she has read to her children, tucked and re-tucked them in several times, reassured them that what they saw was just a prank, only then does she return to pull up the living room shutters entirely. The car is gone but it left a deep, muddy semi-circle of tire marks on the grass. Farther up on the lawn, in bright white letters, upside down to her, so that passers-by can read, has been painted the word *KILLER*.

Laura goes to the bathroom window later; it also looks towards the front of the house. She looks to see if she misread what the young man had painted. She must have. She had looked so quickly and it was upside down. Laura's mouth is still filled with mouthwash when she lifts the shade. Betsy is in her front yard. On her hands and knees, bare handed. She is yanking out clumps of grass.

She can't remember when she and Betsy had stopped being friends. She'd not even had the opportunity to tell Betsy that Mark had left her until weeks after it happened. It was a garbage night and Laura had been back and forth to the curb, rolling her garbage cans and recycling bins, something Mark had always done, and now the chore had become a ritualistic marker of yet another week's passing.

Mark's seemingly unobtrusive departure—he packed some bags and loaded up his car while she and their daughter watched their son play soccer—had in reality plunged her into the deep end. By garbage night, she'd felt submerged in her grief, like a drowning victim. She knew she was losing to her despair and dislocation, that she was struggling for air. It left her feeling fuzzy. She might soon forget even to hold her breath.

Betsy had just stepped onto her own side door stoop and bent down to sort some recycling.

"Hi," Laura managed to say. She struggled to answer when Betsy asked how she was. "Um, not so good. Mark moved out." And there was some relief, to share this fact with someone known, but removed from the immediacy of her pain.

"What? I don't understand."

"He told me one morning that he had stopped feeling loved and needed. That this..." she turned and pointed back to her house, "no longer felt like home."

"But..." Betsy stopped and actually hugged her, "you've made a beautiful home. You're a wonderful mother."

"Apparently not."

"That's not fair. Is there another woman?"

"Yes."

"Then that's just his, well, 'you know what' talking."

"Maybe, but what do you do when everything you've worked towards, when the thing that is, well, you know, the only thing that you've made, when someone else decides for you, that thing no longer matters, maybe never mattered."

"He doesn't get to decide that."

"But what if he does, it feels like he did."

"Laura, nothing has changed. You are those children's mother. You have been there for them twenty-four seven. They need you. Nothing else matters."

"But Mark wants the kids to live with him half the time. He says that I should get a job."

Betsy shook her head. She gave Laura another hug.

"Please let me know if there is anything I can do."

But they had almost no contact after that, except for another brief exchange.

"Owen's going to be around more, for a little while." Betsy said.

"Oh."

"He's taking a break from school to figure out where to focus his studies. So he can help you with the yard, or moving heavy things. Just let me know."

Laura began to see Owen going out the side door. He would walk the family dog at mid-day, when everyone else his age would still have been away at college, or working a retail job. Wearing headphones, he hardly looked up from the sidewalk. She finally caught his eye one day when he was in the driveway, and she waved. He took the headphones off.

"Hey, Mrs. Tucker."

"Hi, Owen. You know you don't really have to call me that. You're all grown-up and, I guess, I'm not really Mrs. Tucker anymore."

"Yeah, my mom kinda told me that." He smiled uncertainly.

"I hear you're taking a break from school?"

"Yeah, things weren't going so well with classes."

"That happens." Laura's turn to smile. "Did you like any of the classes in particular?"

"I had a great English professor, but...I don't know."

"You could take some classes, you know to keep up. The community college is getting good reports these days."

"I don't know."

She got him to talk a few other times, Owen shifting his body weight from one foot to another. But in their last few conversations his voice was weary. She began to feel that even her comments about the weather or the dogs might feel intrusive. After that, Owen stopped taking off his headphones.

Still, she continues to hear the Carter's life when she opens any of her windows. They converse, apparently, only when in different rooms; Betsy's big, turned-up-at-the-end voice questioning, motivating, curdling in its effort to reach her children in the far corners of their house. Laura has always sensed that the family's loudness humiliates Owen. But then, one day, it was his own agitated voice that passed through the exterior walls and landed, like a hurled brick, at Laura's feet. She had paused on the sidewalk in front of their shared driveway. She'd been walking her dog, as she does methodically every day, at the same time, so as not to require intention. The dog was peeing.

"You don't understand what it feels like. I can't get it right. I don't know how to be," Owen talked loudly, but it sounded choked and hollow.

"Honey, we can help you," Betsy said.

"You don't understand. It's...I don't...It doesn't feel like it will ever change. You can't fix this."

Laura had felt so nosy, even though that time, she'd not been given a choice.

Even more, it made her want to speak to him, tell him in a way that wouldn't seem inappropriate, that she too is in the middle of a scary stall, like a plane that has lost an engine. That for her, too, what was supposed to be life's steady movement in its intended direction has gone suddenly off course. It feels unfair. And she panics at the thought of tomorrow, and, the day after that. Does it hurt that he can't turn his fear into strength to step in a new direction? She cannot. Not even a small step, in any direction.

She's been near the kitchen window more often, hoping to find Owen walking out or back in again. She'll go outside and tell him that he can talk to her. Just like he used to. But he's nowhere. His car never moves from its spot at the top of the driveway. The other Carter cars continue relentlessly to pull up behind Owen's and to back out and away again. It must feel awful, being left behind. The way she feels in the misspent hours before the kids get home, even after she has made the beds and stacked the dishes, walked the dog, returned phone calls, answered emails, and organized the kids' schedules.

Tonight, Betsy has come home early. Laura watches as she juggles overstuffed grocery bags from the trunk of the car, her penetrating voice moving into the kitchen before even her body or the bags have made it through the side door.

"Owen? Sweetheart? How was your day?" She sounds upbeat but aggressive. "Everyone will be home soon. Can you come and help me unpack? I'm making your favorite." Laura is sure she hears the exhale of a groan, the faint whisper of "Please...leave me alone," escaping through the bricks.

She is at the kitchen island later that night, laptop opened, reading her email. The children are out for dinner with their father. She has had several glasses of wine and has picked at some leftovers from the refrigerator. Her fingers are itchy on the keyboard, as if they intend to do something without her permission; she has googled the Carters. Nothing appears and she pushes down the top of her laptop. It feels unseemly, like she is spying. But before it snaps shut, she pulls it back up again, and types, in addition to the name, the name of their county, and "drive by shooting." It's not an accurate description of what has happened, but it feels close.

The only thing she finds is a story about an incident a few weeks before, at the Brickman family farm in the very north part of the county. It had happened late in the evening. Two friends were shooting at bottles. The family kept guns for hunting. A young man, the grandson, nineteen years old, shot another young man, a friend, age twenty, who later died at the hospital. The shooting was determined to be accidental, and no charges were filed.

What a sad and pointless way to die. She clicks on a couple of related links but they seem to have no relevance. Laura goes again to shut her computer, feeling still like she's done something wrong. Betsy's parents, Laura remembers, have a farm house somewhere not far from here. The Carters often go visit. Then she remembers Betsy's maiden name.

She wants to demand the Carters tell her. She deserves to hear it from them. At least the angry young man has not returned. And the pit parties have stopped for the moment. She understands now, maybe. Betsy's attempt to pull Owen back from the edge. To tell him in her own fabricated way, that it was not his fault that his friend died. They can pretend it didn't happen. Life goes on. But how can Betsy believe that? Pit parties will not save Owen. He, of all people, will see straight to his mother's fear. And he will feel the unfairness. That the dead boy's family had not gotten the chance to shield their son, or help him to smile again.

She is back at her window, desperate to reach out to Owen, somehow. Her damn dog knows how. No matter how much she has neglected him, he will flop in front of her, force her to look into those soft eyes while he exposes his belly, all in a way that says, "I know you are doing your best and no matter, I still love you." She could be Owen's mother, she is old enough. Instead she feels his age, on that scary precipice where life can barely be imagined, but still with too much time for self-judgment. Worrying that things might get more awful or, just maybe, better. She has it worse, so many more years in which to count up her failures. If she could just let him know that she sees his pain, acknowledge that it is big and ugly, but assure him that he is strong enough to hold it and she will not turn away. But Owen remains a ghost, inside.

She sees Jack pulling out of the driveway, taking his youngest son somewhere. Then the Carter's daughter drives away. For the first time in months Laura knows what she wants to do and she is moving. Moving in the direction she intends. She walks through her kitchen, out the side door, and across their shared driveway. She'll go through the Carter's side door, march up the stairs and let herself into Owen's room. But before she can reach it, she sees Betsy sitting in her backyard on one of her "fun" chairs, staring at the charred remains of an old pit fire. Laura turns and lets herself into the gate. Betsy looks up at the sound of the latch clinking. Her eyes are so sad, she does not throw on her regulation smile. Laura realizes how much more comfortable that feels. She approaches Betsy, cautiously, as she would approach a cat loose in the neighborhood not sure if it's just lost, or it's panicking. Perhaps it is Betsy who really needs her.

"I know what happened." Laura says, Betsy looks confused but then her shoulders sag with her exhale.

"It was an accident," Betsy says.

"That's what the papers say."

"The papers?"

"Well, online."

"Oh, it's online?"

"How is Owen?"

"He was already depressed, now he won't move from his bed. I'm worried he might be suicidal."

Laura winces. "I didn't know, I mean I can see something is wrong..." she trails off.

"I can help," Laura says a few moments later. "I can stay with him if you need to get out and I can talk to some neighbors about helping with dinners or errands."

Betsy is shaking her head vigorously, but wordless.

"Everyone gets sucker punched sometime," Laura says, and Betsy's agitation slows. Laura has a chance to glance up. Owen is at the window, looking down at them.

About the author:

Lisa Battalia is a writer, mediator, attorney, and the mother of two teenagers not fully launched. In a transitional, mid-stage of life, her writing often speaks to experiences of stuckness; unexpected moments of clarity; and taking first steps. She was selected to participate in the Jenny McKean Moore Writers Workshop at George Washington University, and was recently accepted to the MFA in Creative Writing program at Queens University of Charlotte. Her "Three Day Wind" was selected for inclusion in an anthology of women' writers "Aspiring to Inspire," published by Durham Publishing in March, 2014. She was also awarded runner up in Minerva Rising Literary Journal's 2014 chapbook contest. Her story "The Gift" has received several honors—honorable mention in Bethesda Magazines' 2012 Fiction Contest; 2nd place in Rough Copy's 2010 Short Story Contest and was published in the 2013 Summer/Fall issue of New Purlieu Review. She self-published a novel "The Warming Season" in August 2013 and is currently working on her second novel.

ROYALTON ROAD
©2017 by Michelle Wotowiec

"Mitch!" Mr. Lee's voice breaks into my world. "Mitch, wake up."

He started calling me Mitch last summer after we spent the evening together down by the pier. Instead of opening my eyes, I keep them closed and I try to remember the smell of the heavy North Carolina air that afternoon. I try to remember the way the wet sand felt on my bare feet. It was cold, wasn't it? You were back in Ohio wearing your gray hoodie that looked like it was damp but wasn't. It just looked that way. You are probably surprised that I remember that hoodie. I hear the girl behind me snicker and I close my eyes tighter. I am back by the pier again. The pier went 700 feet into the ocean and it was the day that guy from Oak Island caught the 42-pound, 5-ounce kingfish. He caught it before we got there, so we didn't actually get to see the fish. But that catch, the big catch of the season they said, was why everyone was celebrating down by the water.

I was careless after Mr. Lee and I drank several hard lemonades on stolen beach chairs. The dead weight I'd carried on my shoulders for so long simply evaporated into the ocean mist. You should've seen his smile and the way his thick salt and pepper hair accented his jawline. I couldn't help but smile as he tried to cheer me up.

"What's Emily Dickenson's favorite reindeer?" Mr. Lee asked in a very serious voice from his beach chair.

"I don't—"

"Dasher."

Come to think of it, it was the first time I laughed since you disappeared.

That moment, sitting on the chair with Mr. Lee, letting the waves come up to our toes and his smile—God, his smile—I didn't even think about you. The excitement of it all is why I got a splinter when I ran up the stairs. I know you probably think it's dumb, but I felt so beautiful that night, in my white flowing skirt and rainbow bikini top that I thought I could fly. I was flying. It was the splinter that slowed me down—my blood running into my fingers when I lifted my left foot to my right hand as I leaned against the wooden railing smeared with fish guts. Mr. Lee, in his defense, looked legitimately concerned when he saw the blood drip to the ground.

I know you don't want to hear what we did that night, so I won't tell you. I will only say that it is exactly what you didn't want to happen.

"Mitch, are you planning on sleeping through the entire class?" His voice is deep and I try to imagine the way it sounded that night in the hotel room, but I can't. It isn't the same voice. I figure I have pushed my limits, so I peel my right cheek off my arm and sit up in my chair. The kids to my right continue to whisper and snicker and I want to throat punch them, but I don't.

"That-a-girl. Now who wants to tell me the name of Ernest Hemmingway's first novel?"

You weren't always right, you know. Like the time we sat at the pizza shop over on Detroit after we snuck out of your uncle's house. What were we doing there? Killing time, you said. You said that we wouldn't have much of it—something about those minutes back then, you said they wouldn't last. I didn't realize you were talking about the minutes in relation to us spending them together. I thought you were talking about some sort of apocalypse or something. I don't know why I thought that. And while you were right about our minutes being finite, you weren't right about the pizza. You said it was the best pizza you ever had. I can still see your hair tucked behind your ears and the papercuts on the right pointer finger that you had me kiss. I thought the pizza tasted like cardboard with pre-sliced packaged yellow American cheese melted on top, but I didn't tell you that. Oh, and the mushrooms were definitely canned. I just smiled while you went on and on about what our future might hold together. We could move down to the lake and raise cattle. Happiness, you said. We would find that on a farm of our own when we could wake up at the crack of dawn together and milk our own cows. We could be cattle farmers, you said. Ha, can you even imagine that?

"You need a ride home?" Mr. Lee asked after he walked past me in the school parking lot. I was angry by that time. Angry at you. Angry at my parents. Angry at the weather. I was just angry. So fucking angry. And in my defense, at that time I had never thought of Mr. Lee in that way. This was before our trip to the pier. And besides, he was old. Remember, the conversation we had about how old people tend to forget they exist? Forget that time continues to move and they find themselves living in the past? We imagined old grandpas rocking in beat-up wooden rocking chairs, reminiscing about their boyhood all through the night while their wives fed the cats and did the laundry. Up to this point, I had placed Mr. Lee and everyone else his age in that category. The aging. The dying.

"You wouldn't mind?"

"No, not at all," he smiled. I followed him to his dark blue convertible.

He took a quick look over his shoulder before he started the ignition. Magic 105.7 played The Everly Brothers' "All I Have to Do Is Dream."

"What do you want to listen to, Michaela?" he asked, lowering the volume.

"This is fine," I told him while I pulled the seatbelt over my shoulder and across my lap.

His car was clean, unlike yours. It looked as though he had just taken it through the wash and hand-vacuumed the floors. I asked him to put the top down and he obliged. He didn't make a move that day. A sleazebag would've made a move right away, you know? We drove the fifteen minutes down Root Road in silence, feeling the wind on our faces. He dropped me off in front of the house and gave a quick wave before he drove away.

Do you remember that weekend you and I spent together driving through Maine in your old white Jeep? You had just gotten your license. I don't know if I ever told you, but there would be a time later in life, long, long after the era of you, when I would go home with a guy who drove stick and would regret it for years. I didn't know that then, though. I just knew you drove stick shift and there was something real about the way you looked at the highway while we talked about my childhood and where I came from. I told you about the hours I would wait by the phone for my father to call and how those hours didn't follow the rules of time. Each minute felt like twenty as I stared at that phone, willing it to ring. How the phone that once rang every Friday stopped ringing entirely. If you were here today, we would laugh about how much technology has changed things. How sitting by that stationary phone stole time from me. Forced me to stay and take up a specific amount of space. It made my world stand still—that damn home phone with the spiral cord. During that trip, the stories about my father just fell out of my mouth and into our air and next thing I knew, I was in love. The kind of love that can only be found in a white Jeep driving through Maine with you. Things have changed a lot—you know. I eventually stopped waiting for him to call. And in fact, when he finally did call, I didn't even answer the phone.

I think back to that weekend now, how we slept together in the tent on the shore and the way your hands felt when they made their way up and down my back, my stomach, my legs, my neck...and I realize that I never asked you any questions.

I couldn't figure out why you did it. That might have been why I was so angry. Angry? I know, I shouldn't have been angry. I should have cried when I heard the news. I should have thought about all of the things in my life that mattered most to me:

1.

2.

3.

(I will fill these in later when I figure out what matters to me).

I couldn't do that. I couldn't cry. I was sitting on the hill, cross legged, looking at the stars when my mother told me about the accident. She said *accident*, so I didn't entirely understand the weight of the situation until later. I didn't believe her—wait, were you there when she told me? Did you see the way her lips pursed together like a child's and how her shirt was only halfway tucked in? She was always in a hurry. Of course I didn't believe her. I was under the impression that when things like that happen, time stops. Something changes. The world where I am existing takes a second to breathe—to sigh—and I would feel it. I would feel it. Feel something. So, no, of course I didn't fucking believe her.

The last time I saw you was about a month after our most recent breakup. You were in Strongsville Square looking at the Christmas lights. It was quite the display—bridges and trees and posts and snowmen all covered in hundreds and hundreds of tiny blue, red, and green lights. Do you remember? I had just left the mall with Kim and Laura. Laura spotted you from afar, sitting on the bench on Royalton Road. I did a double take to make sure it was you, and then before I knew it, my legs were bringing me toward you. Onto your lap. Wrapping you in my arms. What are you doing you asked me. Missing you I said. That is when you looked at me the way you used to look at me—the way you looked at me in Maine—and I was sure that things were going to be okay.

I had read too many romance novels where people can read each other's minds and I just assumed you understood that we were going to try again. We would be in love again and things would work out. We could make those minutes infinite after all. Then we left you there on the bench and I swear you had a smile on your face. Or at least that's how I remember it.

Mr. Lee began taking me home regularly. I'm not entirely sure how it happened, but one day I looked at him and he was handsome. His sharp jawline and kind blue eyes made me feel a certain way and I wasn't entirely sure why. I wasn't sure why. He started to tell me about his childhood and how he was raised in New York City. He said that things were so different there – people were so fucking busy all the time. Things moved so quickly. Like living in fast-forward, he said. Can you imagine that? Living in fast-forward? He didn't like it, but said he didn't know any different until he took the job out here in Ohio. It was a last-minute move, he said, after his daughter died (I know, it was sad, I didn't even know he had a daughter). He said his wife left him and the bank was about to fire him, so he decided to up and leave and teach a ninth-grade English class at Brunswick High. He said when he got here that he felt like he found his soul for the very first time. He said he breathed in a way that he had never ever done before and he fell in love with our countryside. With our endless fields and shallow rivers. When he placed his hand on my thigh one Wednesday afternoon after the second stop sign on Firestone Road, I let it stay there. That's when our thing officially started. You have no right to care though, you know. I am only telling you because I want you to understand that I am not some sleazy girl fucking her teacher just to fuck him.

He had been taking me home for two months before he finally kissed me. I was waiting for it, if I am being honest. I was dreaming about it. He took a detour on River Corners Road and stopped his car down near the Millers' farm. There's no traffic down there, you know. He stopped the car and looked at the street for a minute as if deciding whether or not to cross a line that couldn't be uncrossed. Then he turned his body toward me, placed his hand on my neck, and pulled me in to kiss him. You know what was weird? He tasted nothing like I expected. I somehow expected him to taste old. Or stale. Or heavy. But he didn't. He tasted like raspberries and summer air.

You were wearing baggy Jencos and a black Volcom tee shirt the first day we met. It was Mr. Fechuch's class – do you remember? It was halfway through the school year when you moved to town. You walked in ten minutes after the bell rang and so you had to deal with the embarrassing introduction and the surprise poem Mr. Fechuch makes everyone read when they come in late. He said to break you in, he wasn't going to let you slide by (although, if I were you, I would've made the argument that it was your *first* day and to give you a break). You had no idea what the fuck was going on, but you smiled and read from his piece of folded up yellow paper about raging at light dying, days closing, and going ungently into the night. And then you laughed and you did a bow.

You didn't realize it, but every girl in the room fell in love with you at that very moment. You were *so* handsome with your dark thick hair pushed forward and to the side. You sat behind me because it was the only open desk. We made eye contact as you walked past and you would tell me that was when you knew you would never be the same. You told me that was the moment you fell in love—really fell in love—for the first time. You claimed time stopped, but if I am being honest, I didn't feel it stop (although, in a moment of passion, I know I told you that I felt it stop that day too—I am sorry I lied to you).

So here I am in Mr. Lee's class feeling like a fraud. I am sure everyone knows that he and I had a thing going—I overheard Kim talking to the new girl about it in the bathroom. They didn't know I was in the stall. *Slut* and *fucked-up* and *disgusting* were a few of the words that felt heavy in my ears.

It was at the end of that pier in North Carolina with Mr. Lee when I finally talked about you.

It was after I got the splinter on the pier and Mr. Lee carried me down to the shore to put my foot in the salt water. He carried me in a way that made me feel safe. "You knew that boy, Jeff, didn't you?" Mr. Lee asked as the waves splashed at our feet. Maybe it was endless horizon or the setting sun that made him think about you, but that was the first time he had brought it all up to me.

"Yeah." Then just like that, you won again. You wouldn't fucking let me escape. I was so tired of carrying you in my head. So fucking tired.

"I'm sorry. Going through something like that has to be hard on you."

Silence.

"You can always talk to me, you know," and there was something sincere in his touch as his pointer and middle fingers traced a line down my spine.

I let him take me to the hotel room. It was after we finished when time finally stopped. I closed my eyes and was surprised when I found myself back on Royalton Road. This time, though, Kim and Laura weren't there. And this time I didn't let my legs lead me to you without my knowledge. I saw you sitting on the bench and took my time getting to you. I took my time and I never do that. It was this patience that allowed me to see that you were crying. You were sitting on that bench in front of the large display of Christmas lights, crying. That was when I knew it wasn't about me. It was about that sadness you fought from deep inside you every single day. The sadness you tried to kill with your smile. With your laugh. With me.

About the author:

Michelle, who currently lives in New York City with her husband and three cats, has worn several hats since her writing journey began over a decade ago: daughter, sister, student, waitress, secretary, professor, director, fiancé, and, most recently, wife. Her realistic fiction is inspired by her diverse experiences and the spirited people she has encountered along the way. She takes pride in being introspective and looking for the common humanity we all share, regardless of where we come from—the little things that connect us and have the power to inspire kindness and understanding.

"Royalton Road" explores what is left behind when we unexpectedly lose someone and what it is we do with the pieces still remaining. One reader called Royalton Road a "love letter". Michelle didn't intend for this to be the case, but very much likes the idea that it was interpreted as such.

Michelle's very grateful to have the opportunity to once again publish with Scribes Valley Publishing.

Michelle would like to thank her husband for showing her an entirely new existence in which she has found love and support in a way she previously believed to only be found in fiction.

A THOUSAND MEMORIES DEEP
©2017 by Sarah Evans

The fog pours downwards to fill the crevasse. I am a thousand metres high, knee deep in snow and rooted to the spot. I need to move on.

I don't look down as I turn round to face the upwards slope. Fresh drifts are already covering my earlier tracks.

The hut is close by; it has to be. It might as well be on another continent.

I won't find it, not today.

I won't make it through an exposed night.

I'm going to die up here, alone.

These along with another million screaming thoughts clamour for attention. I need to not pay any of them heed. I breathe in frosted air and focus on step-by-step survival.

What the fuck are we doing? I am not going to hear you saying that.

The light fades, reducing my fog horizon down to nothing. I cannot continue.

I make for the closest cluster of rocks. They rear abruptly upwards and provide no concave shelter. I drop my rucksack. My fingers are clumsy through Hi-Tec gloves as I unfurl my four-season sleeping-pod. I bump down into the give of snow, release ice-block feet from boots and plunge them into the padded taper of my bag. I grab for cloth remnants—spare knickers and shirts, a microfiber towel—and fill up all the niches. I expose fingers of one hand to zip myself in, as far round as I can, and I curl up tight against the rock, like a fat grub.

Blackness engulfs me, I cannot see beyond its absoluteness. I hear nothing other than the wheeze of my own panicked breath. Seconds pass in a slow eternity with no means of tracking.

I have to stay awake.

I have to keep on massaging my gone numb toes.

I have to keep on clenching and unclenching muscles in a bid to stop my blood from freezing.

We'll never survive the night in this. I am not going to remember how you said that.

I jerk awake to cold exhaustion and there's a two second delay before awareness floods back in, just how screwed I am.

I long to drift back down.

I long for the bliss of oblivion.

I tighten everything against the slide.

The dark has lifted, though only slightly. I feel the wetness of fresh flakes on my lids. I need to move, to discover a spring of energy from within my empty store. *We'll never find it, not in this, not if we've lost the path.* I need to bury the memory of you saying that.

The walk was only supposed to take six hours, and yesterday I walked for almost twice that. I cannot be far from my destination. My body surges with primitive instinct. I unzip my snow-encrusted bag; wriggling out takes gargantuan effort. I stuff numbed feet into ice-stiff boots. Everything takes several ages and a day. Impenetrable grey swirls before me. The snow has got deeper. I don't know where I am. The hut is my only hope. I have no means to find it.

My water bottle is solid and I nibble at snow. My lips freeze. I play battle with a tube of high energy gel, the top refusing to yield and I feel like crying, frozen tears, I feel like giving up, giving in, curling into a snowball in the snow.

The tube opens in a splurge of sugar and minerals. My tongue coats in cake-mix and my throat refuses to swallow.

I reroll my sleeping bag—ineptly—and attach it to my rucksack.

I stutter forward. Each step requires more power than I possess. Each step and I am more lost.

We need to turn back. I am not going to recall how that was what you said.

The light fades; darkness closes in. I have followed a series of switchback loops, aiming to cover the nearby surface area. I have made no progress. I am off-path with no means of regaining it. I have no idea how near or far I am from the only possibility of rescue.

If only the fog would lift and the snow stop falling. If only I could find the hut. If only I had listened. *If only*s stretch to infinity.

I am at the end of the day; I am beyond the limit of energy and will.

We need to let people know our plans; I need to keep intruding thoughts at bay.

Several lifetimes pass. I fight against sleep and cold, and it's a battle I cannot win.

Memories seep in through semi-slumber.

A heated argument amidst the blizzard. Both of us yelling into the wind. And the moment you turned your back, determined to win the debate one way or another, intent on heading down, ignoring my held-firm opinion. *After all you've been so frigging right all along.* The path was steep and narrow. Sheer rock rose one side and an impossible slope slipped away the other. Your tall figure faded into grey.

I shudder to consciousness amidst an approximation of light. I shake my head clear. Today is my last.

I am on the knife edge of survival.

I need to find the hut.

I need to avoid repeating ground in circles.

The wind blows hail against my goggles and I can see no further than my feet as they shuffle step by freeze-frame step. I don't want to die. I want release from pain and tiredness.

Lesser grey separates out in a fleeting eddy.

I glimpse a glistening expanse below. Flat and smooth.

My heartbeat quickens: the hut overlooks a lake.

The view disappears.

I stumble steeply down across rough ground towards the come-and-go glow.

Even if we find it, what then? I close my ears against hearing you say that.

It rears up out of nowhere. Black amidst the white. Sharp manmade angles.

Yes! Triumph surges through the near collapse.

It is twenty impossible metres away. My weight drags. I slip and slide and stagger, until... My gloved hand reaches out to test the solidity of my mirage. I trace a circuit: smooth walls, tightly shuttered windows. I spot steps, nine-tenths buried, an impassable hurdle of snow and ice. I summon the last vestiges of strength.

I reach the door, reach for the handle. It doesn't budge.

Come on!

I have no muscle power for busting doors. I yank down harder. The handle gives and I lurch inside. My breath freezes in the still air.

Through a lobby is a large room lined with bunks. The switch does not deliver light. Through the far door is a washroom, the taps stuck solidly in place.

Out of season facilities are basic: I knew that, but still.

The door at the end of a corridor is locked, the window is not. I manage to shove it open. I remove my outermost layers of padding and I wriggle my way through, landing head first on a desk piled with pens and folders. I finger-feel my way towards slivers of light and I crank the shutters open and survey my surroundings.

I discover: a wood burning stove and stack of logs; a Calor gas cooker with battered kettle half-filled with frozen water; a cupboard full of tins and part-used packets of dried food.

I would grin if my lips weren't so cracked and sore.

I remove my gloves. My fingers are turned to raw sausages. The first match breaks. And the second. I cannot afford to break all the matches. Carefully, carefully I strike the third. The gas ignites to a blue flame. I turn to the iron stove and I never was good at this sort of thing. I am extravagant with the kindling and firelighters—not thinking beyond the moment—and crouch down and watch; my concentrated hope will ensure that the flames will catch.

Does anyone actually go near the hut in winter? I block that you ever said that. Try not to remember how fierce my determination was to do this. How the trail was a lifetime's dream and I loved the idea of crunching along it in the snow; the paths could get overcrowded in summer, so I'd read, and I didn't want to be part of some fair-weather tourist motorway.

Flames dance off the logs, splurging out a heady heat which leaves me greedy for more. I drink lukewarm water from the kettle; hunger competes with starvation-nausea as I spoon up semi-heated beans from a pan. My fingers throb. My body aches. My feet are consumed by white-hot flames and I cannot bring myself to remove my socks and take a look at my toes.

A thousand thoughts are hammering in my head but I need to retain focus. A black box sits in the corner. I know enough to recognise a mountain radio. Have never used one.

It can't be that difficult.

It will come with instructions.

The first turns out not to be true and the second is no use because the instructions are not in my language.

The face of the radio is covered with dials, levers, buttons and switches. I recognise the on/off symbol. Inhaling wood-smoke air, I flick to *on*. I hear a static whine. I tap the microphone to hear the feedback. 'Hello?' I say. 'Hello?' My voice echoes round the small room.

I fiddle with buttons and dials. I stare at the unfamiliar labels, as if willpower might unscramble meaning.

No one's going to come looking, not when you refused to tell anyone where we were headed. I try to shut you out, try not to remember how I accused you of always wanting life to be so tame, of not knowing how to act spontaneously on the moment, how I thought that not being accountable to anyone was part of the adventure, that it made us free.

It is dark out. I can sleep, safe in the knowledge I will make it through to tomorrow.

I snuggle down into my sleeping bag and then heap on covers from the warden's bed. I am a million times warmer than before, yet I cannot stop shivering, my body clinging to the memory of what it has endured. My feet itch and scream to the point that I wish them back numb. My mind pounds, memories batting against my weakened defenses. Every time I ease down towards sleep, I startle awake again. Thoughts slip through. The memory of that evening in a bar, a group of fellow travelers from the local hostel, all tanked up on beer and tales of daring.

'I'm planning to walk the trail,' I said, winning admiring smiles.

'People do that in winter?' you asked, and your eyes met mine and I felt that shiver of desire.

The day passes with a different quality of slowness. I bask in relative warmth and available food while my brain runs through OCD concerns. How long the fuel will last, how long the food, how long my sanity?

I count and recount the tins and packets, rearranging them in different piles alongside my own meagre supplies. I perform elaborate calculations in a childish scrawl, the best my swollen fingers will allow: calorie count per item, multiplying up then adding, estimating a normal daily intake, then reducing—by a third, a half, three-quarters—and now I'm into long division and it feels another me who once upon a time did this sort of thing in school. I stare at the answers.

Is it better to starve quick or slow? To die of hunger or of hyperthermia?

This is all your fucking fault. I'm not sure if it's your voice I'm hearing, or my own.

I spend the days amidst a plethora of plans, seeking options based on my own self-reliance, rather than the chancy response of others.

I don't see that we've any option, you said, arguing that we should return. We wouldn't have enough light to make it all the way back down, but losing height would at least gain us a degree or two of warmth; it might take us below the cloud-line. 'We'll be fine,' I insisted. 'We're almost there.' The blizzard was closing in but I wasn't going to give up so lightly.

We were no more than five ordinary hours of walking from the safety of yesterday's small village; it felt like we'd worm-holed into another universe.

I fiddle with knobs and dials and switches in the hope that—like a monkey with a typewriter—I will finally hit on Shakespeare.

I rearrange my supplies. I devise my means of escape, improvising snowshoes from firewood and string. I dismantle one of the bunks and contemplate how the metal tubing might serve as poles. I picture packing up essential supplies, bundling myself up and heading out onto the mountainside and—this time—keeping to the path which will lead me down to safety. I block the thoughts of how bitter it is outside and how much it hurts to stand. Within thick socks, my toes are encrusted with black scabs. I can do nothing for them, other than endure their pain.

You'll end up back in the same nightmare; it's your voice that I hear, as clearly as if you were standing at my side, though you never said that.

Days pass, followed by their nights. My body has thawed; snow buried memories threaten to thaw too. I cannot let them.

Not yet.

I wait for rescue. I wait for slow death and wonder if dying on the mountainside might not have been kinder. I try not to think.

I will not think how you were heading away. Leaving me behind. How convinced I was that the only way through was up and on. It had to be. The hut couldn't be far.

I will not remember how I lunged towards you, determined you would stop and listen and turn around and come with me. I slipped...

I pile on clothing and brace myself to go and poke around outside. I fill the kettle with snow. I discover snow covered solar panels and water-logged twigs. I fail to discover the line of the path. I wave my arms and shout into the void. I take a pole and scratch a large SOS into the pristine white above the lake then scatter ashes scraped out from the fire into the grooves. I test out those snowshoes which fall apart within a few metres.

Each time, I return, teeth chattering and exhausted. Each time, I vow never to go back outside, not ever again. Each time I am back within my enclosure, I know I cannot simply sit it out. I oscillate between conflicting certainties.

You're always so fucking certain that you're right. I must not think of you saying that.

The stash of food diminishes; I recalculate a lesser ration and hunger gnaws at my insides. The pile of logs is reducing down to ash; I am feverously cold. Why not stuff myself silly and be done with this chilled rationing, going out on a blaze of warmth, getting the whole thing over with more quickly?

The Calor gas gives out.

I read and reread pages from the warder's single crime novel but words blur and fail to cohere into meaning. The pounding of thoughts becomes more and more insistent. I am slipping into lunacy. I can barely stand to stand and I long to take a hatchet to my toes. Mornings arrive as dim smudges of light; I pass through the hours of semi-day, willing my final days to pass. Dark falls with a blackness that is unnerving. I try to sleep for as many hours as possible, try not to notice how the glacier closes in, how my small pocket of warmth evaporates so easily. I try to sleep and not to dream; I try not to think.

The *not think* thought is buried a thousand metres deep; I cannot face its resurfacing. *I don't want to die up here*, you said.

Time suspends and yet days and nights accumulate to an imprecise number. I have not kept track like all good prisoners should. Each day, my absence lengthens and rescue becomes more likely. People will have noticed I am gone. They must be scouring the area, will discover the chain of hostels and cheap hotels we stayed in. The guy who offered us a lift up to the pass will come forward. They will home in on the trail and then the hut.

The logic feels thin; aloneness feels all consuming.

I try to hold it back, but death fills my thoughts and perhaps demise is not so bad; it's where we all end up, after all.

The fog in my mind presses closer. The fog outside lifts, revealing a clean, crisp day, sunlight sparking off the snow. And then...

The *chak-a-chak-chak* slices through, distant and then growing closer.

Yes! I head out onto the top of the steps and yell and wave my arms. I retrieve a brightly coloured throw from inside and try to use this as a flag. The desire to live floods through, coursing strongly through my veins. *Here I am! Come and get me!*

The helicopter comes into view. It circles away.

No!

No!

I yell more loudly, as if my own small clamour might be heard between the silence of the mountains and the ear-split of the propeller.

The noise gets louder, it fills my head.

The helicopter hovers above before descending in a blast of noise and air.

Time speeds up. My senses are in overload. People come towards me, speaking an unknown tongue and I jabber in my own language back. Gloved hands reach out to touch me. Kind eyes peer out from fur-lined hoods. 'OK?' the man says.

'OK.' I repeat back the universal word. I am not OK; I'm fantastic.

He says something and he has to repeat it several times before I recognise my own name and I am smiling and nodding before my smile fades and my head shakes, warding off those other sounds I don't want to hear. My arm is firmly gripped and I am steered towards the helicopter. A glove presses on my head, ducking it safely beneath the rotating blades. I am bundled inside. Strapped in.

We take off. We are flying up into the sky and I'm abandoning my past, looking only towards the future. I don't watch out of the window, do not want to see the land I so carelessly thought would be a once-in-a-lifetime experience and all the more spectacular for being snow-tipped. We would get away from the crowds, immerse ourselves in the fairytale landscape, simply existing, you and me amidst the beauty, reconnecting to the earth and our inner selves. Being authentic.

OK, if it's what you want, you said. You gave up battling against my convictions.

Time hangs and I want to stay here amongst the thrum of noise and warmth of people, remaining high, high above the ground.

We bump down to a bone-jarring landing. Strong arms help me out.

I find myself immersed in bright, suffocating heat. The white-coated staff are kind, their fingers gentle as they remove my socks and prod my in-agony toes, before bandaging them up. They check out my pulse and reflexes. They measure and weigh me. They conclude things between themselves, then smile at me.

I find myself in a different bright-lit space. Two police officers sit across from me and a translator is at my side.

I stumble through my story, pausing after each sentence to allow the translator to render my words meaningful to the stone-faced officers whose eyes are hard with skepticism, whose repeated questions are designed to tease out falsehoods, to trick me into saying something else.

I listen to myself and wonder quite how plausible my story sounds.

Are you sure you know what you're doing? I am not going to remember you saying that.

I am taken to a nearby hotel. My passport is lost and I've been warned not to try and go anywhere.

I have no desire to go anywhere.

The hotel room is sauna hot and I turn the thermostat up higher still.

A phone sits by the bed, but I have no one to ring. My mother died a year ago and I have nobody else close. For twelve months I have felt adrift; the trip was supposed to bump-start me back into feeling alive. *Both of us orphans*, you said, forming part of the instant connect between strangers.

I order room service, far more than I can eat and I bathe in the surfeit of heat and food. There is nothing but the aching of my toes as distraction and it is harder, ever harder, to keep out unwanted thoughts.

The space is white. Lights flash and dazzle my eyes. Sweat drips down my arms and my face glows hot. I am confronted by a sea of journalists and their million unanswerable doubts. A translator sits one side and a cop the other.

The translator speaks under-voice, letting me know what is being said, but I close my ears to the back and forth, until the questions home in on me.

I explain, for the thousandth time, just why it was so impossible to hike back down from the hut.

Yes, it was only supposed to take six hours.

Yes, the conditions gradually improved.

No, I didn't feel able to attempt the descent.

Yes, that continued for thirty days.

No, I wasn't trying to hide anything.

I explain, for the thousandth time, how we were lost and that you slipped.

'I don't know how it happened,' I say. 'One minute he was there and the next I heard him crying out as he fell.'

I will not picture how I slipped and stumbled. How you broke my fall, then fell yourself. How you slid and then slid further before stopping, clinging on with gloves and boots above the crevasse. How your eyes met mine.

I am clinging on to the edge of thought. I am hoping that if I can hold off from thinking for long enough then at some point certain things can no longer possibly be true. I am burying the memory, like your body, a thousand snowflakes deep, in a crevasse that no one will ever find. I am burying the look of horror in your eyes as your foothold gave.

About the author:

Sarah Evans has had over a hundred stories published in anthologies, magazines and online. Prizes have been awarded by, amongst others: Words and Women, Winston Fletcher, Stratford Literary Festival, Glass Woman and Rubery. Other publishing outlets include: the Bridport Prize, Unthank Books, Riptide and Best New Writing. She has also had work performed in London, Hong Kong and New York.

BY INVITATION ONLY
©2017 by Mike Tuohy & Celeste Woody

Credit card. Credit card. Time share. Sweepstakes. Past due notice for my ex-husband's Camaro. "Mother! You said there was something from the government for me."

Mama glanced at the intricate water stain on the ceiling. She refused to paint over it since the Guatemalan lady who helped her with housework after the hip surgery said it resembled Jesus. When Mama moistened her lips and tensed, I knew she was fixing to tell a little lie, a sin she did not take lightly. "Oh, it was nothing."

"Mama! I told you about opening my mail. It's a Federal offense."

"Well, it looked important, but it wasn't." She unplugged the percolator and lifted the metal filter basket.

"I think I can make that determination. I'm thirty-one, not seventeen."

She pursed her lips and rocked her head. "I know. You're all grown up and don't need a man."

"Mother, my mail!"

"Don't take that tone with me, young lady. Besides, I already put it in the trash."

To Mama, rooting through garbage fell outside the limits of proper behavior for a lady. The sole justification for such action would be a certainty that one's wedding ring had fallen inside. Retrieval required stout rubber gloves and a bowl of hot bleach water standing by. My sister and I laughed about that incident for decades. Mama never found it funny. We knew to let it go once Daddy died.

"If you're not going to tell me what it's about, I'm going to have a look for myself."

Her eyes widened as I yanked the lid from the white plastic trash can. One arm struck out like a cobra as she flung the contents of the percolator basket on top of the egg shells, newspaper, and junk mail.

"Mother, I'm a nurse. Coffee grounds will not deter me." I reached deep and pulled out a dripping mass of envelopes, coupons, and slick brochures adorned with bits of her last couple of meals.

Mama turned away. "Dear Lord!"

"I'm getting a post office box tomorrow!" I eyed one festive envelope with faux handwriting and abundant exclamation points. "Unless I win one of these sweepstakes and get my own house."

Mama busied herself, putting away cutlery from the dishwasher, an appliance she mistrusted. She inspected each fork tine, spoon bowl, and knife blade for spots or residue. One of four went noisily in the sink for remediation. "Settling down would be good. All of your classmates have."

I made an unladylike snort. "You thought it a good idea when I settled down with Randall."

"You should have given him a chance."

"If you recall, Mama, his girlfriend gave him plenty of chances while I worked at the hospital."

"He seemed so nice." Her voice trailed off like a runaway party balloon.

To Mama's mind, my failed marriage reflected poorly on her. She never let me forget I owed her a respectable son-in-law. Someone like my daddy. She failed to understand they quit making men like that right after World War II.

"Mama, I'm not proud that my most permanent address consists of a wicker fruit basket in your kitchen. I'm leaving Florida and taking that job in Texas. Get me my own mailbox with a lock on it and—"

A brown envelope that looked like official business clung to a slimy melon rind. When I touched it, my mother sucked her breath.

"Department of Corrections? I don't know anybody in prison. Maybe some that should be." Laying the soggy paper on the countertop, I gently tugged out the single page letter and read aloud. "In accordance with the Victims' Rights provisions of Florida Penal Code, you are hereby notified that appeal has been denied in the case of—"

Mama snatched the document from my fingers like an experienced cotton picker. She must have donned her yellow rubber gloves while I dug. With Kabuki theatricality, she tore the page into a dozen strips, wadded the mass into a ball, and pushed it deep into the refuse, tamping it down with her fist.

"Now that's the end of that!"

"Mama! You have no right!"

"I am your mother. It is my duty."

The garbage slowly rebounded, releasing an invisible cloud of fetid air. I stepped back. "Mama, just tell me what it was about."

Working the faucet with her elbows, she rinsed the gloves before pulling them off and draping them over the edge of the dish drain. "Do you want to watch a man being electrocuted? Do you really?"

"Of course not! Why would you ask such a thing?"

"There was a man who bothered you once. I just pray they will soon make it so he can never bother you again."

I sank into the breakfast nook and considered her words. 'Bother' hardly described what that man had in mind but Mama held strong opinions about language and unsavory subjects. Long-suppressed images flashed in my mind and a hollow sensation took over my gut.

"Could you turn the disco down? Nobody's here to dance."

The perkiness drained from our waitress' face. She plainly

thought me a bitch.

My companion, Cheryl, grimaced. "We want to talk."

"Got it. Two margaritas and kill the party." She sneered as she pointed us out to the bartender. The music volume dropped just a little.

I shrugged. "Don't suppose she was expecting a tip anyway."

Cheryl tilted her Farrah Fawcett hair in the direction of the front door. "There's something for you, Angela. Bet he's a doctor."

A particularly handsome man with wavy brown hair approached the bar. Waiting for his drink, he scanned the room with a discerning eye, his gaze coming to rest on us. Cheryl noticed and touched up her already perfect Ferrari-red lips before downing the rest of her Margarita. I knew this move. She wanted this man to buy us drinks.

Cheryl tapped me with her toe. "Nothing leisure about that suit. Doctor. Maybe plastic surgeon."

I stirred my ice. "I doubt he wants to talk shop with a nursing student."

"So you didn't take Miss Tampa. You took swimsuit. For God's sake, Angie! You starved yourself six months for that damned pageant. You're good as you're ever going to be. You've earned this!"

The stranger looked better and better as he approached our table.

"He has his eye on you, Cheryl. You going to tell him you're getting married next week?"

"I'm keeping my options open."

I gave her shoulder a light punch. "Shame on you!"

She winked at me and turned toward the stranger, giving him the slutty smile the pageant coaches warned us never to use on stage or near a camera.

He responded with a tight-lipped smile. "Mind if I join you ladies? I could use some tips on local customs."

Cheryl nodded as if hypnotized.

I felt a need to intervene. "She's getting married next week. Her fiancè is an accountant."

The stranger's left eye twitched but he kept his gaze fixed on Cheryl. "Lucky man. Hope he appreciates your stats."

He delivered each word like a gift. Cheryl accepted them with shameless pleasure, bearing the same expression she had when Jeff presented the ring.

The stranger took her hands. "I would like to show you what it means to give your life to a man."

I expected Cheryl to toss the icy remnants of her drink in his face. Instead, she stared into his eyes, her lips moving slightly as if miming his words.

I cleared my throat. "Cheryl! Aren't you supposed to pick up Jeff at the airport?"

She shook her head and blinked as if awakened from a spell. "Sweet Jesus! Jeff!" She gathered her belongings and dropped a ten-dollar bill on the table. "See you next week, Maid of Honor."

We both laughed as the man looked on, eyes darting back and forth as if tallying up our relative merits.

Cheryl held out her hand, drooping at the wrist. "It was nice meeting you."

"The pleasure was all mine." He took her hand and kissed it, then pulled her close.

Cheryl pushed him away and stepped back, knocking over a stool. I tried to read her expression. I saw her slap guys who tried to kiss her at football games and throw a rock at her boyfriend's car as it peeled off after a bad date. They stared each other down, breathing as if just finishing a sprint.

The man smiled innocently. "Sorry. I just couldn't resist."

Cheryl smiled back briefly, then looked down, over at me, then back at him, "No harm done. I just have to go."

"Can I walk you to your car?"

Cheryl blushed, something I had never seen her do. "No, no. I'm right out front." She turned to me and we embraced. She whispered in my ear. "See if you can bring him to the wedding."

I cackled and pushed her away. "Get out of here!"

The man's head turned slowly as he tracked Cheryl's progress all the way to her car. When she pulled out on the Gunn Highway, he turned to me and smiled. "I'm Ted. I didn't get your name?"

"Little Runner-up, evidently."

Ted tapped my arm. "Don't be like that! You're a beautiful lady. Your friend just had that look of a woman in peril. I can't resist a gal in trouble."

"I have plenty of troubles." Regretting the words as soon as they left my mouth, I waved to the waitress for the check. The music volume had been creeping back up and I had no desire to stay.

Ted leaned in close. "I'm an attorney. Maybe I can help. Let's go somewhere we can talk about it."

Having kept men at arm's length for most of the past year, I wanted to sink my fingers into his dense dark, curly hair and pull him to my bosom but the good girl in me still ruled. "I beg your pardon? I don't know you."

"I feel like I've known you all my life. Bet you're an Aries."

I pinched my necklace just behind the little ram pendant and jiggled it like a tiny bell. "I don't suppose this gave me away?"

Ted's lower lip pushed out briefly like a wet slug. The smile returned. "Busted! I'll bet you've heard them all before."

I felt my face flush. "I don't really do bars but, yes, it's all the same old lines." Funny how the way he looked in the three-piece suit made me long to see him out of it. I extended my hand. "I'm Angela."

He nodded slowly. "Angela. Yes. I can picture you as an angel."

The check came. He made no move to pay it. I put a ten on top of Cheryl's, glad we stopped at two Margaritas, not that driving troubled me. After ten years of Cecchetti ballet I could drink three more and still walk a straight line on my tiptoes. "I need to get home."

Ted touched my wrist. "I'll walk you to your car. Lot of creeps out there." He wielded that smile like a shepherd's crook, his gaze like a tether.

"I can take care of myself." I grabbed my purse and dug out my keys, making sure the little can of Mace lay near the top of all the crap. "But, thanks. You hear about those girls up at FSU?"

Ted winced and shook his head. "Horrible. Terrible thing." He examined his fingernails. "So young."

As we walked to the exit, he placed his hand at the small of my back. With the sun setting, I was glad for his company as we walked toward an unlit corner of the parking lot.

Approaching my crappy little Vega, I reconsidered Ted's offer. "So, where is this place you wanted to go?"

He grinned like a little boy. "Just a little north of town. Peaceful. You'll like it."

I considered my evening plans. Doing laundry at my mother's house. Listening to her complain. Going home to fold clothes and get ready for school. I needed to live a little.

"I can only go for a little bit. I have an early class tomorrow. Anatomy."

Ted stroked his chin like some kind of guru. "Happens to be my favorite topic. Come on. My car's just over here."

Prickly shrubs along the passenger door forced me to enter from the driver's side. An older model Impala, the front seat was roomy and the vinyl slippery. Before I could pivot to put my feet on the floor, Ted reached under my skirt, ripping my pantyhose. I pushed and he advanced.

"Back off!" I shoved as hard as I could, pushing Ted onto the pavement. I hit the horn with my elbow as I exited.

An older couple getting into a car a few spaces away turned and looked at us. Ted stood and gave them a little wave. "Just a little misunderstanding."

I jabbed his chest and spoke in a low voice. "I'm not that kind of woman."

"Sorry, Angela. I've just never been so close to such beauty."

"Don't feed me that! You don't touch a lady like that, unless you are a doctor."

"Did I say I was?" He sounded unsure. His upper lip and right eye conspired in a twitch.

"You said you were a lawyer. Is that true?"

"Trust me, I know my way around the law." He smiled and touched my hair. "Look, Angela, I'm really sorry."

He reminded me more of a little boy caught stealing cookies than a rapist. I turned to our audience. "It's okay. Just teaching some manners." The man nodded and helped his wife into the car. As they drove off, I faced Ted. I knew it was wrong, but had never been so turned on. "Got a cigarette?"

Ted looked puzzled for a moment. "Think I saw some in the glove box. Let me check."

A little odd. Every smoker I ever knew kept a running mental inventory of his supply. He returned in a few minutes with a flattened soft pack of Kools. He broke two before succeeding in getting one out whole for me.

I laughed. "You don't smoke, do you?"

"I've been meaning to take it up. Somebody left these."

"You don't know?"

"Hitchhiker, I guess." He struck a match and cupped the flame with his hand against my cheek.

My first cigarette in almost a year. I was through with pageants. Too much self-denial. I was ready to make up for lost time. I looked up at Ted. "Aren't you going to have one?"

Ted shrugged. "They make me cough." He looked away, then right into my eyes and spoke in a throaty whisper. "What I really want to do is burn a candle for you."

"What do you mean? Like at midnight Mass or something?"

"Just come along. It's a quiet place where we can relax and get to know each other."

I mentally ran through all the warnings I heard since puberty. What men were after. How they lied to get it. What evil they could do. My curiosity remained, demanding satisfaction. "Let me follow you in my car."

There went that twitch again, followed by the smile. He leaned in as if for a kiss but left me wanting. "Fine. Just stay close. It's a little remote."

***

Heading northwest out of Tampa, the Gunn Highway soon narrowed to two lanes flanked by orange groves. Five miles on, doubt started to overtake lust. Something about Ted troubled me. The very qualities that made him irresistible now made me suspicious. Too quick. Too presumptuous. Too damned good looking to be real.

After Daddy died, I dealt with many lawyers: clever, conceited, aggressive sons-of-bitches. Hitting on me, a teenage girl while they were supposed to be protecting Mama's assets. Arrogant, opportunistic, self-serving bastards. I could see it in Ted. Then again, he seemed unsure whether he was a doctor or a lawyer. Who could forget whether they had been through four years of law school or twelve years of medical school and internship? Either way, why was he driving an old Impala? He should have a Mercedes. He could not possibly be a lawyer. Probably not even a real Ted.

The red tail lights suddenly flared as if angry. I braked too, hoping Ted had not read my mind. Why should I doubt this beautiful man who simply wanted to burn a candle for me? He made it sound poetic, even romantic. He plainly wanted me. Or did he? At no point during our encounter, even when he ran his hand up where it did not belong, did he take his eyes from mine. He never even tried to kiss me. Even with my limited experience, that seemed odd.

The Impala made an abrupt left onto an unmarked dirt road. I followed and stopped just a few yards off the pavement. The dome light came on and I could see Ted's eyes in the rearview mirror. He held up one thumb. When I returned the gesture, the Impala took off.

I started slowly, keeping my gaze locked on the taillights. They reminded me of the eyes of an unholy beast. They drew closer together and I had to floor the gas pedal to keep pace. Seventy. Crazy on such a narrow track in the wilds. I eased back on the gas just as the red lights dropped and disappeared. I reflexively hit the brakes, fishtailing to a stop in loose sand. I considered the possibilities as my panic rose. Canal. Sinkhole. Cliff. This last gave me pause. Not many cliffs in mostly flat Florida. When the lights emerged a little farther away, I realized I had left out *dip*.

Hyperventilating, heart pounding, I cursed my foolishness. The red eyes blinked long enough to break the spell. My rational, sensible self came back. No more behaving like a teenage girl. What was his rush anyway? Doctor or lawyer, he could do better than taking a woman out into the woods. He was probably married and could not bring me home. Jackass. Time to go.

With my Vega nearly sideways across the narrow road, the drive wheel spun uselessly in the soft sand of the shoulder. To my right, I could see the Impala's headlight beams jerk and bounce as Ted made a five-point turn in the narrow track. Though I knew better, I floored the gas pedal, succeeding only in going deeper. I longed for my daddy's old Mustang with the V-8 and Posi-traction. I tried another approach. Reverse. Forward. Reverse. I almost made it out of my own hole on the second try.

The Impala dropped into the dip just about the time I broke free and fishtailed back onto the hard-packed road. I hardly slowed as I turned onto the Gunn Highway, causing a tractor-trailer to swerve and brake hard. When the driver tried to pass, I sped up. I wanted it back there; a buffer and a witness. The truck got on my tail as if to make a point and stayed there for a couple of miles. I saw no sign of the Impala until the road widened to four lanes and we came to our first red light. I considered running it when Ted pulled around the truck and stopped beside me. He leaned over and rolled down his window. Lacking functioning air-conditioning, mine was already down.

Wild-eyed, he screamed at me. "You're a crazy woman!"

"Sorry! Changed my mind. Going home. I have electricity. Don't need any candles, thank you."

Ted slapped the steering wheel. "You bitch! You fucking bitch."

The light changed. I pushed the gas pedal to the floor, wishing my little four-cylinder would try harder. Ted kept pace for a couple of blocks, shouting insults until we passed a police car waiting to pull out of a convenience store parking lot. Ted took a left at the next intersection. The cop car's lights started flashing but it took off in pursuit of a speeding motorcycle. I went on to my mother's. Though I lived nearby, I did not want to be alone just then.

By the time I reached the front door, my hands shook so much I dropped my keys twice. "Damn it!"

Even mild cursing seemed to draw my mother and she did not let me down. She opened the door slowly, at first wearing the look that usually preceded the lecture about demon rum but she quickly put her fingertips to her mouth. "Honey! What happened?"

I broke down before I could speak and she led me to the kitchen table, providing tissues and a cup of her cure-all tea. After I told her the story, at least as much as I felt I could share, she placed her hands over mine.

"He did not harm you in any way?"

By *harm*, I knew she meant *violate*.

"No, Mama. It wasn't like that."

"But he followed you back? He threatened you?"

"He had this look like, I don't know, a crazy man."

Mama sighed. "Honey, we need to call the police about this."

"Mother, nothing really happened. I mean, it's not like he—"

She held up her hand. "Doesn't matter. That man assaulted you. Lord knows what else he had in mind."

I stared into my teacup. "He said he wanted to burn a candle for me."

Mama put down her cup and tilted her head. "Whatever could that mean?"

"It sounded kind of sweet when he said it, but now—"

She stirred some sugar into her tea. "Doesn't sound right to me. You think he might have been one of those drug-crazed hippies? Like Charles Manson?"

"No, Mama! I would never have gone off with someone like that. He was well-dressed. Well spoken. Said he's a lawyer. He'll probably sue me for libel if I file a report."

She patted my hand, went to the phone, dialed 0, and asked for the Tampa Police. I knew better than to argue.

After a few transfers and choppy conversation, Mama put her hand over the mouthpiece. "A Detective Mitchell wants to come by and get your statement tonight."

I sighed. "Can't we do this in the morning?"

She repeated my request and listened. "He says this man is probably out looking for you or another woman right now."

I thought about my car being out in the driveway. I put my mother in danger now. "Tell him to get his ass over here."

Mama gave me a stern look. "I am not saying that." She spoke into the phone. "We would be delighted to see you tonight. Do you prefer tea or coffee?" She hung up the phone and eyed me critically. "You really could use some freshening up."

"Mama, don't try to turn this into a date."

"Furthest thing from my mind. Not that it should matter, but you might want a more modest skirt when speaking to the detective. At least some fresh hose."

The reminder made me queasy. "I had some slacks in my laundry."

She nodded approval. "In the dryer. Nice and warm."

After changing, I joined Mama in the living room to watch television. She developed an interest in the local news since my beauty pageant turned into a soap opera. The original winner relinquished her tiara and sash to pursue an acting career, moving me into second place. Questions remained regarding the new Miss Tampa's eligibility.

The lead story concerned a plane crash.

Mama looked at me with raised brow. "Now that's interesting."

"Good Lord, Mother! You aren't hoping Miss Tampa was on board?"

"Heavens no! Though, if it's God's will that you move up, we should not question His methods."

"I don't want to get the title that way."

"Well, there are other pageants coming up. You're a beautiful girl and you've worked very hard. You deserve recognition."

"I'm through with pageants, Mother. I'm two semesters from graduation. I'll be getting a job soon."

"You'll be getting a husband." Her eyes widened. "Hand me the remote. I can't stand to hear another thing about this."

Tallahassee policemen, Florida State troopers and FBI agents dominated the screen. I plucked the remote from the coffee table and turned up the volume. "I want to know if they have a suspect."

"—the Florida State University coeds were members of the Chi Omega sorority. The assailant is described as white male with brown curly hair, approximately thirty years old. He remains at large. The Federal Bureau of Investigation has provided this photograph of a man they describe as a person of interest."

I only saw the photo for a fraction of a second before Mama turned the TV off. The image remained suspended before me. The hair may have been a little long and unkempt but the nose, chin and cocksure smirk were the same. More than anything, the shot caught the man looking right into the camera. I knew those eyes.

"Mama! That's the guy."

She looked at me and then the blank television screen. She turned the set back on. By the time the picture returned, a smiling man in a tacky suit brought a sledge hammer down on a car windshield as a bikinied blonde woman tore a giant price tag in two. The voiceover proclaimed that Crazy Bob would be smashing prices all weekend.

"Honey, are you absolutely sure?"

"Mother, I sat at a table not two feet from that man just this evening."

Mama sat down and sank back into the sofa.

"Are you alright, Mama?"

Her mouth trembled. "I only turned it off because one of those girls looked so much like you."

I happened to be in Mama's carport when the mail truck pulled up. I pushed the wheeled trash bin in front of the kitchen door and hurried to the mailbox. I wanted first shot at the delivery this time.

Mama bumped the screen door hard against the bin. "Oh, for Pete's sake!"

I recognized the Department of Corrections envelope immediately. I culled it and my bills and handed the remainder through the gap in the door to my mother. "Sorry, Mama. I just could not allow you to interfere with the postal service again."

She pursed her lips. "I was not going to do any such thing."

I pushed the bin aside and stepped inside. "Of course you weren't." I read the letter and dropped it on the kitchen table. "Execution's back on. I've been re-invited."

Mama glanced at the ceiling, now more apparitional stain than not. "Lordy, I wish it would just be over."

"How did I even get on the list of victims? It's not like he—"

Mother interrupted. "You know, that man caused so much mischief they probably have a boxful of reports on him. God knows, once they caught him, no reason to sort it all out. Once you get on a list, nobody asks why ten years on." She busied herself with the remainder of the mail, dividing it into three piles before discarding it all.

"You know he killed that little girl a few days later." I swallowed hard. "I should have done something more."

Other than the distant sound of the approaching garbage truck, things were quiet in the immediate vicinity of my mother's house for most of a minute. I welcomed Mama's interruption, even if it started with a gasp coupled with an unladylike belch. It was nice to know she was moved.

"What could you have done? Just be glad the Good Lord was watching over you."

"I'm sure He saw plenty."

Mama sat upright. "Whatever do you mean by that?"

As I stared into the page, the letters merged into an impressionistic face. There were those unblinking eyes. That cocksure smile.

"You know, Mama, seeing him in that suit, I actually imagined spending the rest of my life with that man."

"Honey, if you hadn't turned the car around, that *night* might have been the rest of your life." Mother sighed and stirred her tea. "I suppose you can't be blamed for wanting to go, for 'closure' and all such as that."

"Well, what would you do in my position, Mama?"

My mother closed her eyes. "In your position, I believe I would just skip it and try to forget, maybe even work on forgiving, as Jesus would want." Leaning forward, she looked into my eyes and pounded the table once, rattling the silverware. "But if that man harmed my little girl, I would want to throw the switch."

I pictured the scene. Nobody looks good in a jumpsuit, especially orange. The thick dark hair shaved to the scalp, there would only be those eyes. Florida still used the electric chair. Sometimes, things did not go so well.

"Mama, I work in a hospital. I see enough death in a day to last me a lifetime." I wadded up the paper and let it fall. "I believe I will decline the invitation."

Mother bit her lip and embraced me as I puzzled over her words. "Mama, what do you mean by 'forgiveness'?"

The whine of the garbage truck two doors away brought her to attention. "We don't need to discuss this anymore." She stood and yanked the trash bag from the can. "Ever!" She cinched the half-full plastic bag with a double knot and pulled it tight.

I held the screen door open as Mama rushed through and hollered to the driver to wait up. The smiling, brown-skinned operator put out his hands. She waved him off and heaved the bag into the back of the truck. She ground her palms together and pointed to a red-handled lever. The operator nodded and engaged the compactor while Mama looked on, her lips pressed into a thin, grim smile.

About the authors:

Mike Tuohy was born in New Jersey in 1954. Moving to Georgia in 1965, he has sopped up Southern Culture ever since. A professional geologist, Mike works the environmental consulting rackets by day and writes at night, making friends, family and co-workers nervous as he chronicles the preposterous through short stories, novellas and a novel. Seventeen of his short stories, including a Pushcart nominee, have been published. A two-time finalist in The New Yorker Cartoon Caption Contest, he has a total of nine words in that prestigious publication. Mike lives by the North Oconee River near Jefferson, Georgia.

Celeste Woody was born in Birmingham, Alabama in 1954 and moved to Atlanta, Georgia where she spent most of her childhood and teenage years. Throughout high school and college Celeste maintained active interests in dance and music, studying ballet and singing. For a while, she sang, wrote songs and toured with the rock band Xanadu. Attending the University of Virginia and the Florida Hospital College of Health Sciences, Celeste has been a registered nurse for over 40 years and currently works at a major hospital in Dallas, Texas. Celeste continues her education, pursuing a Master's of Science in Nursing.

THE EXACT MOMENT
©2017 by Catharine Leggett

Essie pedals past the playful screams of children in backyard pools. *Marco. Polo.*

The light, dim under the canopy of trees arcing the road, the air softened by descending dusk. Past ancestral homes with stately porches, on through the suburbs with dwarfed tree features and hidden underground cables, the hum of air conditioners. Past strip malls with "For Lease" signs, fledgling gyms, rent by-the-hour motels and 24/7 variety stores. Until the city gives way to fields of corn and hay, a lone farmhouse, and the land yields the caress of breezes, sweetened with summer's ripeness.

She pedals through her thoughts: Money. Aqua fit. High blood pressure. Gaining weight. Bernie. His diagnosis. His failing zest. A time bomb. Possibly. Waiting. The dryer on the fritz. The garden to weed. Tomorrow's dinner. Then the day after, and the day after. Dinner, dinner, dinner, dinner. Lunch with Norma. A multi-course offering of her terrible life. The kids. Emily still looking for work. *Mom, I promise I'll pay you back.* Carson. He never calls. Better things to do. Better people to do them with. She understands, but couldn't he force himself occasionally? Dutifully practicing the law of parental selflessness. A big lie if ever there was. What about her? Doesn't her life count? Yard work. Rooms to paint. Bernie less able. Her back. Not bad now, thank god. Knees, too. She must take care. The infrastructure collapsing. Time winding down. Memory lapses. People ask, what do you do now that you've retired? She tends to others. She gives. They take. It's not enough, she thinks, until she short circuits, and escapes to a place where she can breathe and see the world from a broader view.

She'd no intention of coming this far. She checks her watch. Gone an hour and forty-five minutes. It will take her as long to go back, maybe longer. Bernie might worry. If he notices; if he doesn't fall asleep in his recliner first. When she headed for the front porch, she left him glued to his favorite show, *Power and Politics*, following every word blond-haired, dark-eyed beautiful Amanda said, her deep-red lips dancing around her perfect white teeth as she voiced her strong political opinions. So certain, so confident. Bernie's superhero. She always made him smile.

Her generation made it possible for Amanda to talk with unbridled authority. Essie and her contemporaries did all the heavy lifting, broke new ground, thumbed their noses at convention and got called names. Feminists. (Nothing wrong with that.) Butches. (Nothing wrong with that, either.) Bra burners. (They can be uncomfortable, especially the kind with underwires.) Women's libbers. (You are right. Thank you.)

She should turn back, and she will soon, but now that she's in the country she wants more. More space. More air. The possibility of continuing. A break from everyday tedium, the ties of sickness and aging, for just a little while longer.

Her restlessness or edginess—whatever you want to call it— came upon her quite suddenly, raised her up in her seat, made her dizzy and hot and her heart race. It wasn't menopause either, that was over years ago, it was something else, something more powerful. And then she knew: it was the last bit of estrogen leaving her body. She looked over at Bernie, his eyes fixed on Amanda.

From here on, without her female hormone, she and Bernie will start to look alike. She's seen evidence of this happening. "Is that a man or a woman?" she asked Bernie as they waited at a light for an aged pedestrian to cross. Now she and Bernie would meet at some neutral rendezvous point, a blend of both sexes. After forty-two years of living together, eating the same food, watching the same TV, breathing the same air, was it any surprise? They'd become territorial too, barking at each other more often now, two creatures occupying the same cage, marking their space. No one got hurt, their skin too thick to puncture; too much has happened. Too much life.

Silence winds around them like a fence, but it's peaceful and familiar and safe, not so much isolating as comforting, and not angry.

Once Bernie snaps out of his Amanda spell and sees Essie's gone, he'll look for her on the porch, her usual spot, and finding she isn't there, assume she's gone across the street to Anne's, as she often does. He understands her occasional bouts of whatever-it-is, understands she must work something out of her system. He knows his illness is part of it, and allows her personal space and freedom. He doesn't want her to be a prisoner of his limitations.

He'll settle back in his chair, probably doze off; it happens more often lately. The cancer might be draining his energy. Not the kind they operate on or treat aggressively, not at this stage, but something they "keep an eye on."

White mist gathers in creek beds and hollows. Gravel crunches with the rotation of the tires. She leans into the motion, pedals and pedals, the sound of her breathing, deep, heavy, regular. A body fully engaged. Dewy space opens all around her, welcomes her, takes her further.

The last of the sun's glow, coming from beyond the horizon, would soon disappear. And here she is wearing no light-colored clothes, nothing with reflector tape, her spontaneous urge to flee the root of her carelessness. What if a car comes from behind? They might not see her. She could be struck, fly off into the ditch, lay there for hours, even days, and no one would notice. She could die. Though it's unlikely since not a single car has passed. She is ashamed of herself for disregarding safe biking practices, especially since she preaches it to others. So, why does she do it?

She knows why: she dares herself to go right to the dangerous edge, it's part of the thrill, a way to shake herself awake.

Time to turn around and go home. She shouldn't have come so far, wishes she was back at home now, watching the last of the news with Bernie. There's only one journey that has one direction, one you can't do over again. The central topic these last few months. But she got herself here, did this to herself, going well beyond the bounds of common sense, and now she must undo it.

Essie dismounts and turns her bike around, examines the distant countryside, striped with haze, the moon illuminating a line of trees in the distance. In the immediate foreground, nothing is clear. She must cycle into complete darkness, keep her focus on the distant light.

She could phone Bernie for a ride. He'd understand and not scold her for her foolishness. But as she touches her Capri pants pocket she discovers she's left her cell phone at home.

She climbs back on her bike and starts the trip back. Her bike wobbles, becomes increasingly more difficult to pedal. She's worn herself out, she thinks. But no, it is much harder to control. She dismounts and pinches the front tire. Flat. And here she is at least ten miles from home, out in the country, improperly dressed for night riding. And no lights anywhere, not even a house she could go into to ask to use the phone.

She starts the long walk back. The continuous line of crickets' trill threads alongside her from deep in the ditch, emphasizes her aloneness, stretches out distance even farther. She shivers, the night cooling with a heavy dew, her perspiration-soaked shirt cold and damp. Stars burn into view, sporadic and dim, one at a time.

Bernie might be asleep in his chair; it seems to happen more often now. Or involved in a documentary, something about science, absorbed into an alternate reality, his way of escaping.

She hears the pulsing whir of a screech owl in the distance, on and off, on and off. From behind, light shines on the road ahead of her. She steps into the road and watches as a vehicle approaches, leans her bike against her, raises her arms in the air and waves down a pickup truck.

She pushes her bike around to the driver's side. A man looks out his open window, his elbow planted on the window frame, and squints at her through the darkness. "Sorry to flag you down," Essie says. "I've got a flat tire on my bike. Could I hitch a ride with you back into the city?"

He opens the truck door and drops down. "Sure," he says. "I'll just toss your bike into the back."

She guesses he is somewhere in his forties. He has a dark beard, and he smells like oil or gasoline. He must work around machinery, farm machines, she supposes, since they are out in the country. His plaid shirt is rolled up at the elbows and his jeans are baggy, a working man's jeans, not the skin-tight kind the city kids wear.

He takes the bike from her and lifts it into the back of his truck, partly filled with large empty cans and branches, and some other junk she can't make out. He is kind enough not to ask her to lift the bike up into the back. She could have, but it would have been a struggle.

As they drive on, Essie feels relieved. Not about herself being stranded—she could walk back to town, though it would take forever, three hours, give or take. Relief for Bernie. She's spared him some worry. By midnight he'd think something was wrong, since she always called if she was going to be out late, and if she had to walk all the way home she would be much later than that. Once she got to the city's edge she'd hail a taxi, but even so, it was still quite a distance. Bernie didn't need more worry, especially not now.

"My name's Wayne," the man said.

"Essie," she said and shook his rough, calloused hand. Was it her imagination or did he grip it harder and longer than normal?

"Essie? What the hell kind of name is that?" She tries to explain it's a family name and abbreviated, but he continues, "Look, Essie, I've got an errand I'm running. I was on my way when you flagged me down. There's a little detour I need to make away from town, not too far up the road. Once I'm done, I'll run you into the city. Sound okay?"

The last thing she wants is another delay, but she can't very well ask him to take her to the city first. He is, after all, doing her a favor. "Okay. Sorry to ask, but how long do you think it will take?"

"Oh, not too long. Maybe twenty minutes. A half hour. Depending," Wayne says, drumming his fingers on the steering wheel.

She examines his large hands, a working man's hands, smells the earthy moldiness of his shirt and asks him if he farms in the area.

"Well, I don't know if I'd call it farming exactly. Let's just say I have aspirations. I've got a few chickens, a pig and a goat. A dog and a cat. Wouldn't call it a farm. Far from it."

"Do you have a family?"

"Never got around to that." He gave a short humph. "Somehow, I managed to skip it."

Wayne slowed the truck and turned right, away from the city. "This is where I was headed. You just sit tight. Won't take long."

She wonders if he has a cell phone and if she could ask to use it. But Bernie would see his name appear and would wonder who was calling. Or, more likely, not recognizing the name, he wouldn't answer it at all, thinking it was a wrong number, or someone trying to sell something. Without moving her head, she glances at Wayne, and imagines he wouldn't be the type to own a cell phone. No wife to call. No kids to keep track of.

She can't see any house lights anywhere, doesn't know this road. It's very narrow, more like a lane than a road. The truck tosses and sways over the track's unevenness, and she is jostled about on the front bench, grabs the door handle to steady herself. Bushes crowd in, scrape the sides of the truck. He doesn't seem to mind. He must know where he's going, since he lives somewhere around here. "Is this a short cut or something?" Essie asks. "It seems a most unlikely road."

"Unlikely, is it?" Wayne makes a sound that could be a laugh.

"Out here in the country we do things a little different. Let me ask you something," Wayne says as his hands play the steering wheel and the truck lurches over potholes. "What are you doing out cycling so late? Look at you. No white clothes. No lights on your bike, just those tiny reflectors on the back fender and those little shiny strips behind the pedals. About as much good as a firefly, I'd say. I would have run you down if you hadn't stood out in the road and waved your arms like there was an emergency. Like someone got hit."

"I know. It was a really bad idea for me to go out so late without the proper gear."

"Well, what if I'd hit you? What then? Ever think of that? I don't suppose you did. I can tell you, I'd be destroyed. I'd have to prove I wasn't careless driving. That's hard to prove since the law favors cyclists. Every goddamn time." Wayne thumps the steering wheel.

Okay, she can see he has an agenda. She'll go along with whatever it is and won't argue. He wouldn't hear her anyway, and she doesn't want to get him any more riled up. Even a sensible discussion would ignite his fuse. She'll listen for a chance to agree with him, then see if she can steer him off topic.

"Well, see, here's the thing. Cyclists figure they own the roads. They seem to think they're meant for bikes. And then you don't even bother with safety features. Not even light clothes. It's like you're flippin' us the bird. You know why? I'll tell you why. You don't care about the drivers. Do you know roads are for cars and trucks? And that's why they were built in the first place?"

"I know that. I try to keep well to the side. I have great respect for road traffic. I know we share the road." She'll say anything to diffuse his argument. He's one of those drivers who would never back down. Toronto had a mayor who thought cyclists were a pain in the ass and refused to make road allowances for them. Maybe that's who got Wayne going. He's probably written letters to the editor, a place for blowhards to sound off. He's kidding himself if he thinks he's inconvenienced by her. He's enjoying himself taking out all his anger against cyclists on her. Just her luck to flag him down.

"I had no intention of going so far. I got, quite literally, carried away." As soon as she says it, she regrets saying literally. It would escalate his anger even more if he had to pretend to understand its meaning. "I just set out, not even thinking. It's such a nice night, I lost track of time. It was stupid of me. Very stupid." How could she be any more conciliatory?

"Well that's pretty obvious, isn't it?" Both hands gripping the steering wheel, he turns to look at her, seems to scowl, though it's hard to tell in the darkness of the cab and his face crowded by thick hair, a shallow forehead and beard. "Where's your tire repair kit? Where's a flashlight? Where's the light on your bike? Where's your phone? Not even a helmet. Seems like a whole lot of stupidity, if you ask me." He inhales noisily through his nose, lets it go out his mouth.

Essie rubs her hands together hard. "You know what, just stop and I'll unload my bike and you can be on your way. You have things to do, errands to run. I've interrupted your night. I'm fine. I know where I am." She says this with purposeful ease, a lightness in her voice to imply nothing is out of the ordinary. She senses something apart from the bike issue.

Wayne finds this funny and gives a quick snort of a laugh. "Oh, you think that's going to happen, do you? After me pulling over and loading your bike, after you stopped me? Oh no, that is not going to happen. I am not going to dump you out here in the middle of nowhere. You're coming with me."

He sounds pleased with himself, his voice taking on more of an authoritative tone. Being in control must be important to him. Is she a captive? Is that what this was all along? Him out looking for someone?

He starts to slow down, then steers the truck to the side of the lane, turns off the ignition and the truck lights. He sits, staring ahead into the pitch black, says nothing for a while, then raises his hands in exclamation and declares, "We're here!"

"Where? Where are we?" She packs the words with all the forcefulness she can manage.

Essie is lightheaded, almost dizzy. She thinks of jumping out, but he would chase her, and if he caught her, he might beat her up. Or worse. She can't think that way. She must keep the fear out of her voice. Not let him think for one single second he has control. "What are you doing?" she snaps.

"Oh come on now, you're not going to pretend that you aren't after something, are you?"

"A ride. I was after a ride." Her voice crunches down on the hard consonants to let him know she means business.

"Oh really? I don't think so. A woman like you out here by herself at this hour. Seems pretty obvious what you're after. You're begging for it; just begging for it." Wayne twists to face her full on, his mouth open in a sneer as he examines her up and down. "You're kind of old, but you're in good shape. Not even all that bad looking. Kind of sweaty, though."

Essie's thoughts scatter, flushed by nerves. She must control her thinking, stay clear-headed. He probably has a weapon, a knife. He'll hold it to her throat and make her take her clothes off. If she screams, who would hear? No, she must stay rational, in control. She faces him, sets her jaw hard. "Start the truck, take me to the city. Right now!"

Wayne laughs. "In a little while, but first you and me got things to do." He leans towards her, touches her arm, then shifts closer and grabs her face, squeezes it, plants his in front of hers. "You can't tell me you don't want it." His breath smells like onions.

No time for hesitation. "Take your hands off me right now! I am a retired police officer and as I got into your truck I got your license number. I also have a tracking device on me. My husband knows exactly where I am. You will start this truck now, turn it around, and drive me to the city. You will do that or you will go to jail." She says this emphatically, hopes he doesn't detect the quiver in her lies. She waits for him to move, but he sits staring at her.

She glares back for critical seconds, seconds that could make all the difference, his indecision balancing on this exact moment. "Get going I said," she says with fake gravitas, her hands gripping her capris to stop the shaking.

He slides back to his seat behind the wheel and stares out the windshield, as if he is trying to make up his mind about something.

She is relying completely on his stupidity. Her story has so many holes and inconsistencies, surely he'll figure out she is lying. And if he does, it would make him angrier.

He raises his hand and turns the key in the ignition. He turns the truck around, they head back to the city in silence, until she says, "Stop here," at the first strip mall they come to. She jumps out, slams the door of his pickup, and he drives off with her bike. Roars away so fast she catches only the first three digits of his license plate. She thinks the truck is red, but she's not certain.

She flags down a cab, and when she gets home, runs into the house to get some money to pay off the driver, watches the tail lights disappear down the street.

"I was just looking for you," Bernie says in the family room. "I was out on the porch a few minutes ago, looked over at Anne's but didn't see any lights on." He's been touring the house, shutting it down for the night, the way he always does: lamps turned off, remote controls lined up in a row on the coffee table, windows at the back left partly open, the others latched, back porch light turned off, the front left on for her, coffee ready for the morning. A routine she anticipates every night, that sometimes makes her want to scream, but not now.

"I got involved in my shows, and then I fell asleep. Didn't wake up until a few minutes ago. I was thinking about going over to Anne's to see what you two were up to."

He means, to make sure she was okay. Not to check up on her, though at times she took it that way, but to make sure she was safe. "I went out for a little bike ride and then I went over to Anne's." She would tell Anne later what had happened, make her swear she'd never tell Bernie. Worry would do him no good. He needed every ounce of strength to fight what brewed inside him.

"We sat out on her back deck, and had a couple of glasses of wine. It's a lovely warm night. It seemed a shame to spend it inside. Sorry I didn't call to let you know where I was. I lost track of the time."

She would protect him, spare him the truth, that she was loose out there, riding alone in the countryside, intentionally flirting with danger. And him, with a monster lurking inside him; he didn't go looking for danger; he clung to his routines, comforting assurances that he is still on this earth, still alive, the act of the everyday performed with something like religious ritual, a celebration of the usual. When it came to worldly issues that needed to be fought, Amanda, his superhero, would speak for him.

Tomorrow Essie will tell him she left her bike on Anne's front yard, not intending to stay for so long, and someone walked away with it. He'll say that even on this street, even among neighbors, they couldn't be sure of anyone.

She crosses the kitchen to Bernie and hugs him, presses her head against his chest, hears the steady beat of his heart. She will comfort him for the duration of his journey, their journey, however long that will be. They have become one. It is enough.

About the author:

Catharine Leggett's short stories have appeared in the anthologies *The Reading Place*, *Slow the Pace*, *The Empty Nest*, *Law & Disorder*, *Best New Writing 2014*, as well as in the journals *Room*, *Event*, *The New Quarterly*, *Canadian Author*, and *The Antigonish Review*. Other stories have appeared online in *paperbytes*, *Per Contra*, and *Margin: Exploring Modern Magical Realism*, as well as on CBC Radio. She is a two-time finalist in the Columbus Creative Cooperative Great Novel Contest and the recipient of the Okanagan Fiction award. Her novel, *The Way to Go Home*, will be published by Urban Farmhouse Press and will appear in the fall of 2017. She lives in London, Ontario, Canada and taught creative writing in the continuing studies program for Western University.

CRY ON COMMAND
©2017 by Joe Dornich

Somber, graceful mourning, with maybe the occasional tear or two, that's one hundred. We call it a Dry. Hysterical crying, with the wailing and the moaning and the classic rhetorical questions screamed to the heavens—the *How could you*'s, the *Why now*'s—that's going to cost you two-fifty. We call those, and really any tear-related mourning, a Wet. Some weeks Feldman will assign me nothing but Dries. Others, it will be one Wet after another. Those weeks can be exhausting.

Occasionally we'll get a client that requests the "Grecian Widow." They want to see me insane with grief, destroyed by loss, throwing myself on the casket and threating to jump into the grave. Those can run upwards of five hundred.

Not that I get anything close to that. What I get is ten to fifty dollars a funeral plus tips. Not that anyone tips. You'd think Feldman would at least reimburse me for expenses. Like the mascara I go through after a week of Wets. Like my dry cleaning. *Black doesn't show stains,* he likes to remind me, and yes, generally it doesn't. But when you're crawling through freshly turned earth in a dress already damp with tears, it tends to leave a mark.

The only expense Feldman covers are the forget-me-nots I lay on each casket before it's lowered in the ground. Forget-me-nots, of course, being the official flower of the professional mourner.

Monday, I get to the office five minutes late, but just in time to get nearly tackled by some woman reeling through the lobby. She's young, maybe half my age, and pretty, though it's hard to tell with the wide-eyed look of panic on her face.

"What's with her?" I ask Evelyn, our Receptionist and Bookings Coordinator.

"Failed the Fish Test."

I look again at the woman. She's wearing black heels and a matching, sleeveless dress. The dress still has the tags on it.

Of course.

The Fish Test.

Potential mourners-for-hire don't come in to interview so much as audition. After making them stew in the lobby for a few minutes, Feldman invites them into his office. On his desk is a small fish tank. It's a nice tank. It has colored rocks and a plant. It has one of those little treasure chests that periodically burps out bubbles. And, swimming inside, it has a solitary clown fish.

"This is Nemo," Feldman tells them.

"Like from that movie?" they say.

"Like from that movie," Feldman says.

The fish's name is an obvious and intentional reference. People get it and it makes them feel intelligent. Confident. They smile. They relax a little. In some small way, a bond is formed. This is key.

"Can you cry on command?" Feldman says.

This question comes right from our ad. At the bottom, in bold letters it reads: THOSE THAT CANNOT CRY ON COMMAND NEED NOT APPLY.

They say yes. Every applicant says yes.

Feldman says let's see. Then he reaches into the tank and grabs the fish. "Follow me," he tells them.

They walk into the bathroom.

"Welcome to Nemo's funeral," Feldman says. "You're distraught. Overcome with grief. Let me see it. Lay it on me." Then he drops Nemo into the toilet. Both watch as Nemo swims a few disoriented laps around the bowl. Then Feldman flushes.

Almost everyone fails. I suppose it's the spontaneity or shock of it all. It's too much. People freeze up.

Most people.

"If you can't cry for this fish," Feldman says, "this fish who, less than a minute ago embodied the inane reference you so valued, then how can you possibly cry for a complete stranger?"

It's a fair question.

It's at that point most people grab their things and go.

What they don't know, not that it would help them with their grief problem, is that the toilet's a prop. It's not connected to the sewer. Nemo, the water, all come out of a pipe on the other side of the wall and empty into a bucket. On average, Nemo "dies" four to five times a week.

When I first started working here some of the other employees were quick to praise Feldman's humanity, his respect for God's creatures. But Feldman doesn't kill the fish because he's a humane animal lover. Feldman doesn't kill the fish because he's a cheap bastard.

The woman in black is still outside of our lobby. She's hunched over by the bushes and crying now. Sobbing really. It's a messy, mucus-heavy type of crying. Every few seconds she wipes her face, and then wipes her hands on her dress.

She better be careful or the store won't take it back.

"Sure," Feldman says, walking over, Nemo's bucket sloshing in his hand, "now she can cry. What a waste. Nothing worse than seeing a woman cry for free."

When Feldman first started this business, it was simply about addressing attendance concerns. Maybe the deceased was new to the area and hadn't made a lot of friends. Maybe their relatives were far away, or in some cases, no longer living. Either way a low turnout was expected, and nobody wants a poorly attended funeral.

But soon word got around. Soon it became about more than

just attendance. People realized they could transfer their grief. They could hire someone to provide the requisite amount of sadness and suffering while maintaining their composure. Their refinement. Because when someone dies, the human custom and social obligation to mourn their loss still exists, but for those at a certain tax bracket, there's a level of grieving that is, apparently, unbecoming.

That's where we come in.

Feldman likes to remind us that we're more than professional mourners; we're grief surrogates. That through us, people are able to display their loss. Through us, they're able to pay their respects.

But sometimes I'm not so sure. Sometimes I think I'm perpetuating this myth that people can be insulated from loss, from sadness. Sometimes I think I'm just another way for them to avoid reality.

According to my schedule, I have two Dries and four Wets this week, beginning with a Level III Wet this afternoon. Technically, a Level III is "high-pitched, stuttering sobs with continuous tears," but around the office we call it Chipmunk Crying.

It costs one seventy-five.

The deceased is a Mr. Miles Hoglund, the former President and CEO of something called Hog-Smart Industries. It makes me think of a bunch of pigs in lab coats staring intently into microscopes, though that's probably not accurate.

His service is well attended, which suggests that he was popular with his employees, or that attendance was mandatory.

I'm situated off to the side, next to the casket and a large photo of Mr. Hoglund on an easel. In it he has thick, silver hair and bushy eyebrows. A playful smile. He looks like he was a kind man.

After everyone has settled in, a priest reads a few passages from the Bible. Then he tells us not to mourn for Mr. Hoglund, that he is spending eternity living in the house of the Lord. He tells us our job is to continue to find glory and salvation here, the land of the living.

As he talks, I watch a bird peck at a malt liquor bottle someone has dumped in the weeds growing around a crooked tombstone.

The priest finishes, and then a man stands and addresses the crowd. He's tall and lean and emits a health club glow. His cologne is penetrating.

"Today we say goodbye to a great man. A pillar of the community and the bedrock of our work family. To me, and I'm sure you'll all agree, Mr. Hoglund wasn't just a boss he was a mentor. A father figure really. Because doesn't a father protect and provide for his family? That was Mr. H to a tee. Remember when we had that spat of break-ins and muggings in the common lot of employee parking? Who was it that made sure each and every one of you got a pepper-spray keychain in your stocking at the Christmas party? Even Stephanie Goldfarb got one, didn't you? Where are you, Steph?

Everyone turns in their plastic folding chairs as a woman in a black cardigan slowly raises her hand while lowering her head.

"You weren't overlooked or forgotten just because you don't believe in Christmas. And why was that? Because Mr. Hoglund didn't discriminate. And he listened. Like a good father, Mr. Hoglund listened to his family. When we had a few rough quarters and the austerity measures began to take hold, who heard your concerns? Who, in less than three months' time, reinstituted complimentary toilet paper in almost every restroom? You know, every day I took comfort in the knowledge that Mr. Hoglund was up on thirty-three protecting us, and listening to us. Watching over us. And he still is. He's still up there. Sure, he's up a little higher now, probably playing golf with Reagan, but he's still there. Mr. Hoglund is still there for you. Now, like then, his door is always open. Except now of course you don't have to make an appointment and have Margery escort you on to the executive elevator. So now as we undergo a transition, and I attempt to fill some very large shoes, I want all of you to still feel free to talk to Mr. Hoglund. Discuss your concerns. Share your problems. Try to keep these talks brief, or even better, save them until you've clocked out, but still, don't feel that you have to come to *me* with every little issue. Maybe, instead, allow Mr. H to continue to be the father of our work family. Our father, in heaven. Now let's all give him a big hand."

Then everyone applauds.

Everyone but me.

I just cry.

When people hear about my job the first things they ask are, *How do you do it? How do you cry on command? And so easily? Do you think of sad things?* And sure, some of us do. Some mourners maintain a mental catalogue of sad images. A three-legged puppy. An orphan with a lisp. An orphan, who upon being asked if they'd like a puppy, regardless of the missing leg issue, responds with an overjoyed, *Yes pwease!*

Everyone has their triggers. The important thing is to find what works for you.

Other mourners rely on performance enhancement techniques. They'll rub dish soap in their eyes. Hide bits of raw onion in their handkerchiefs. Some pinch themselves through their dress. Others pluck out a nose hair or two.

Me, I just think about the fact that I'm a fifty-year-old widow, that my late husband had been lying to me for the majority of our marriage, and now, because of that, our business and savings are gone, and my job is to cry at strangers' funerals.

I think of that and I have no problem crying.

The day my husband died he was attending a groundbreaking ceremony for our second restaurant. Just after he and some of the other investors put on the matching hardhats, and stuck their shovels into the ground, and smiled for the camera, Gene collapsed. He had a heart attack. They said he was dead within minutes.

A few weeks later a young man called, asking if I'd like a copy of the photo. The photo of my husband right before he died? Who would want such a thing? I was furious. I called that young man some names I now regret.

Then I called back and asked him to please send me the picture.

I still haven't been able to look at it.

Gene and I met almost twenty years ago. On our first date, he told me his dream was to start a business combining the two great loves of his life. I used to think that at some point I made it to the top of that list, but those first two: Catholicism and Chinese food.

Gene told me he experienced it for the first time while vacationing in San Francisco. He was in some hot and crowded dive in a back alley of the Tenderloin, and after that first mouthful, he was hooked.

Chinese food that is. Not Catholicism.

I've tried here and there to get into it, but I never really developed a taste for it. I think part of the problem's that it was forced upon me as a child.

Catholicism that is. Not Chinese food.

But Gene was so passionate, so determined. His enthusiasm was infectious, and truth be told, I was falling in love.

So, I agreed to help.

Gene and I worked hard, and we saved, and nine years later we opened our first Wok With Jesus.

Our first, and now it seems, our last. Things have been difficult since Gene passed. I've missed the last two mortgage payments and now the bank is talking foreclosure and has started repossessing assets. I tried increasing revenue. I tried coupons and circulars. I tried a deal where kids eat free on Wednesdays. We had some dedicated customers from the church, but then Burton Hoover, our day manager, was arrested. By the FBI. It seems that between greeting customers and politely inquiring if they were "right with the Lord"—a practice I never endorsed—and wishing them a "blessed day" on their way out, he was slowly filling the office computer's hard drive with child pornography. The FBI confiscated the computer and ordered the store closed pending an investigation.

So, the church people are gone, and the investors have pulled out, and any hopes of revenue are a moot point.

I'm halfway home from the Hoglund funeral when I realize tonight's my turn to make dinner. I stop off at the restaurant to heat up a few things. Might as well use what's left before it goes bad. Before the bank takes the rest of it.

We're down to our last wok, and the gas company has cut us off, so I'm forced to use some Sterno cans to cook the food. Needless to say, it's slow going. I wander around the restaurant to pass the time.

I imagine when the bank takes over and this place eventually becomes another Walgreens or Starbucks, the first thing they'll do is paint over the mural.

Before our grand opening Gene commissioned a local artist to paint a mural of Jesus between the two buffet stations. The artist rendered Him in the style of The Last Supper—arms out, palms up—as if to indicate the varied and bountiful array of Chinese delicacies. Or so I assume. Gene loved it, but I've always thought something wasn't quite right. It's the face. The lips are too pursed, and the eyes are too narrow, and the whole thing gives off an impression of judgment. As if He knows our General Tso's chicken is more breading than meat. Or that our Egg Drop Soup comes from a mix. And sure, that's all true, but to me, it's easy to pass judgment when one doesn't have to deal with rising food costs. Not all of us can take a few fish and some bread and feed the masses.

Gene wanted to have the artist come back later and add some scripture. Something relevant. Something about ye eating and drinking in the glory of the Lord. But he never did. I talked him out of it. I thought it was an unnecessary expense and, ultimately, we put the money towards a soft-serve ice cream machine.

The bank took the ice cream machine last Friday.

When the food is cooked, I box it up, and then take one last look around. The desk in the office looks so much bigger without the computer. Hanging on the wall is the first dollar we made. Gene had it framed. On the bottom is a plaque with the date, and this inscription: *The realization of a dream. The support of a best friend.*

I take the frame from the wall, break the glass on a corner of the desk, and shove the dollar into my purse.

Goddamn you, Gene.

When I get home, it takes me another ten minutes to find parking because I have to park in the street. Because there's a Windstar in my driveway. The Windstar belongs to my sister Constance and her husband. It's their RV. I'm sure in its day the Windstar was the height of recreational travel technology, but it's long past its prime. Like a lot of us. Its once gold paint has suffered decades of sun bleaching, and now it more closely resembles the color of un-brushed teeth.

Connie and Warren were in the middle of crisscrossing America when Gene died, so they postponed their trip to attend the service and help out. They've been here ever since. I know they're ready to get back on the road, and part of me is ready for them to go, but I also know Connie is worried about leaving me alone.

Truth be told, I'm a little worried about being left alone.

Neither of us knows what to do, and we're not really talking about it, so until then the Windstar's hulking, leaking mass will continue to sit in my driveway, its back end blocking the sidewalk, its right-side tires ruining my lawn.

Connie meets me at the front door. She's wearing another one of her T-shirts. At some point, Connie's entire wardrobe has been replaced by souvenir T-shirts from the various stops of their trip. Yesterday's shirt featured an anthropomorphic cowboy hat warning me not to "Mess with Texas." Tonight, it's one from their Mount Rushmore trip, with a picture of the monument emblazoned across her chest.

Connie's husband is already seated at the dining room table.

"How are you, Warren?"

"Hungry."

"Well, dinner's right here," I say, holding up the take-out boxes.

"Chinese food. What a surprise."

We spend the first few minutes eating in relative silence, the room filling with the clinking of silverware, and the way Warren chews his food so that everything sounds crunchy regardless of its consistency.

"Have either of you talked to Mindy lately?" I say.

Warren grunts out a lungful of air, and throws his fork to his plate where it plops in a pile of shrimp lo mein with little dramatic effect.

"Did I say something wrong?"

"No," Connie says. "It's just Mindy's new job. It's got Warren a touch perturbed."

"My daughter's selling her body like a common whore," he says.

"Warren, she is not," Connie says.

"She lays with strange men."

"She snuggles them," Connie reminds him, and then to me says, "She's cuddling people. It's a healing practice. Oriental, I think. They say it's very therapeutic. Plus, it's certified."

"It's for the best you and Gene couldn't have kids," Warren says.

Actually, it wasn't so much we couldn't, as we just didn't. There was always the restaurant to think of, and concerns about money. Time got away from us and we just never did. Then at some point, we changed *didn't* to *couldn't*. We both knew it wasn't true, but somehow it made us feel better. I've never told Connie that and I'm sure as hell not telling Warren now.

"Because kids will break your heart," he continues. "Sure, they start off as your little angel, as Daddy's little girl, but before you know it they're all grown up, and then they spread their legs and fly away.

"Oh my," Connie says, putting a hand to her chest, covering Roosevelt and half of Jefferson. "Darling, I think you mean wings."

"What?"

"Wings. They spread their wings and fly away."

"No. I don't. Idiot."

Then Warren stands, grabs his plate, and informs us that he'll be in the Windstar. When he's gone, I ask Connie if she remembers Tammy Newton from high school.

"No, I don't believe so."

"Sure, you do," I say. "Tammy Newton. She was in Ms. Marr's Algebra class with us. Red head. Sort of a heavy-set girl."

Connie shrugs with her face.

"She was always eating *those* cookies, and telling everyone how her great-grandfather founded the company. All of the kids called her Pig Newton."

"Sorry," Connie says. "It doesn't ring a bell. What about her?"

"She's dead. I'm working her funeral on Saturday."

After dinner, I head upstairs and lie down. I watch some TV. The Monday Night Movie is some awful remake of *Citizen Kane* where the title character is even more bloated than in the original, and, for some reason, Scottish.

I change the channel. I change the channel and there he is— standing before a pulpit with his two-tone pompadour and ridiculous goatee, his fat face contorted into a mask of sanctimony—Roland Ravanel.

Ravanel is one of the more successful televangelists preaching something called the Prosperity Gospel, which centers on the concept of Seed Faith. Practitioners of Seed Faith believe they can sow seeds, which symbolize their belief and devotion to God, which, in turn, increases the power of His love, and likelihood He'll answer their prayers.

Even now, Ravanel is pounding a fist to the pulpit, imploring his followers to increase the amount of their seeds, so when their inevitable harvest comes in, it will be all the more miraculous. Then the camera pans over to a giant stained-glass eagle, its wings spread, a golden cross in its talons.

Of course, "seeds" mean money, and "sewing them" means

sending that money to Ravanel's church, and the only miracle is that Gene had been doing this for the last twelve years and I had no idea.

I found out after he died. Gene handled all of the finances—the mortgages, the bills here, the books for the restaurant—all of them. Then when I took over, I learned he'd given away almost everything we had.

I remember in the days following Gene's funeral, being paralyzed at the thought of having to go through his things and the memories and pain they'd trigger, and how, in an instant, I went from that to ripping his jackets and suits from their hangers, and dumping out his dresser drawers.

That's how I found the letters. In shoeboxes beneath Gene's side of the bed were hundreds of letters. All of them from Pastor Roland Ravanel and his Garden of Faith Ministry. All of them congratulating Gene on his devotion, confirming his ever-growing place in God's heart, and compelling him to send more. All of them addressed to a post office box I had never heard of.

I called the Ministry demanding to speak to someone in charge, demanding some answers. I was transferred four times and made to listen to over an hour's worth of upbeat, Christian hold Muzak. Then Ravanel himself came on the line. He told me that Gene's contributions were of his own volition. That it was all perfectly legal. Then he said the amount of seed Gene had sewn over the years had been considerable, and he was undoubtedly enjoying a glorious place in heaven beside the Lord. He said this, I suppose, thinking it would make me feel better.

It did not.

Then Ravanel wished me a "blessed day" and hung up. That's how Connie found me—the bedroom torn upside down, Gene's things scattered everywhere, and me sitting in the middle of the floor, crying and screaming at the phone. She sat down with me, wrapped her arms around my shoulders, dried my face on her T-shirt.

It told me that, "Everything's Peachy in Georgia."

Now Ravanel, microphone in hand, is pacing the electric blue carpet of his stage. He's asking his followers if they're lost, and in pain, and desperate for relief. "Wouldn't you like to know that these sorrows and struggles aren't yours alone to carry?" he says.

The show cuts to members of the audience crying and nodding their heads.

Then Ravanel starts crying too. His expression morphs into a doughy swell of pity, and manufactured tears leak from his beady, black eyes.

But it's not real. He's just aping their grief. He's just capitalizing on their needs, and the hollow promise he can take their pain away.

I spend the rest of the night lying awake, trying to convince myself that Ravanel and I are not one in the same. That our roles, our intentions are different. But I can't. The similarities are too numerous, too painfully obvious. Accepting it is only a matter of time.

It doesn't mean it makes me feel better.

First thing Tuesday morning is a pet funeral. Our rates for an animal service are the same as a human's. Our price point depends on the degree of mourning, the amount of physicality in our grief, not what's in the box. Most animal service clients request a standard Dry, or maybe a Level I Wet—silent, yet streaming tears—but what they really want is some company. As they say their final goodbye to what is likely the last companion they had in the world, they simply don't want to be alone.

Some of the other mourners complain when Feldman assigns them a pet funeral. They think it's beneath them. But not me. I don't mind. The way I see it, these animals were loved as much, and were a part of these people's lives, as any other family member. In some cases, even more so. Plus, I've always found it easier to cry for animals than for people.

When I get back to the office I see Evelyn crying at her desk. At first I think she is considering some work in the field, and maybe practicing her technique. But no. Her grief is real. As she collects her things and puts them in a box, Evelyn tells me she made a mistake with the anniversary mailers.

For an extra twelve dollars, we'll send a remembrance card on the anniversary of a loved one's passing. Evelyn says that in our latest mail out there was a bit of a mix-up. It seems she accidently sent the card intended for the family of Bentley Morris, a golden retriever, to the former home of Bradley Morris, the deceased son of Craig and Susan Morris. I say that doesn't sound so bad. Then Evelyn tells me that Bradley was severely epileptic and died of a grand mal seizure. Then she hands me a copy of the card. It reads: *On this day know that your little Bradley is in Heaven, thinking about you, and wagging his tail.*

Evelyn says Feldman has discontinued the service, and to absorb the revenue loss, he's letting her go. I know she's struggling. Not only is she raising two little girls on her own, but the younger one has some sort of foot issue—no arch, or too much of an arch, I forget which—and has to limp around in a corrective boot.

I march down to Feldman's office but he doesn't want to hear it. He says Susan Morris is some bigwig on the Chamber of Commerce and the word of mouth alone could ruin us. He says an example needs to be made. He says it's out of his hands.

Still, I continue to protest, but Feldman waves a Client File in my face.

"I know you're upset," he says. "Good. Go use it."

Then he hands me the file and tells me to not be late.

It's another rich guy's funeral. Late sixties. Millions in the bank. Died on his catamaran. His four kids from his three marriages are here, but neither of them looks too bereaved about Dad's death. Honestly, they seem a bit bored. The current wife is here as well, though she looks young enough to be one of the kids.

A trophy-wife client always makes for a difficult job. They still want someone else to do the messy work of grieving, but they don't want to be overshadowed, or out-mourned.

Like this one. Even though the wife requested and paid for a Level III Wet, throughout the service she keeps giving me this look. She keeps narrowing her eyes and furrowing her otherwise unlined face as if to say, *Hey, reign it in a little.*

So, I reign it in a little. I give her what she wants. I know my place. I may appear to mourn for the dead, but I cry for the living.

The thing about being a professional mourner is that the job is almost entirely physical, and, over time, that physicality becomes habitual. Muscle memory takes over. It allows the mind to wander.

I think about the people that send Ravanel money, the people that attend his services. Almost all of them are extremely ill, or the loved ones of an ill person. They're hoping to be saved from Parkinson's, or have their paralysis cured, or be free from cancer. They're hoping for a miracle. But not Gene. Gene wasn't sick. Even his heart attack came as a surprise to his doctor. So what was it? What was it about our life that he was so desperate and determined to fix? That he felt he needed a miracle to do so? And how did I not see any of it? What was he looking for, and why couldn't he just talk to me?

When I get back to the office the lights are off and everyone's gone. Evelyn's desk has been cleared of her photos, and postcards, and little knickknacks, and I realize I never said goodbye.

There's a note on Feldman's door saying he's closed early to do some damage control about the Morris debacle. He reminds me that we have a DistaGrieve service in the morning, and that he'll be operating one of the cameras to insure it goes smoothly and one more thing doesn't get "cocked up." How lovely. What lovely language. When I remove the note, the door opens a crack and I see the light from Nemo's tank is on. So I go in and sit at Feldman's desk, and watch him swim for a while.

I never had to take the Fish Test.

Before all of this, before Gene died, and Ravanel, and the

money problems, Feldman was one of our customers. He'd usually come in alone, sit in the back corner of the restaurant, and read the paper—the obituaries of course—while he ate. Afterwards I'd bring him his check, and then he'd ask for a to-go box, and then I would explain the nature of a buffet.

Then one night Feldman came by just after I'd locked up. I was still reeling from the Ravanel news. Burton had been arrested that afternoon. The restaurant was technically shutdown, and I wasn't supposed to have any customers, but I was too tired to care. I let him in. Feldman helped himself to what was left of the buffet, but instead of going to his usual table, he sat with me. He asked what was wrong.

"What makes you think something is wrong?" I said.

"Have you seen your face?" he said.

So, while Feldman ate, I told him everything.

At first, he didn't say anything. He just sat there, playing with the remnants of his beef and broccoli. "Huh," he finally said. "What is it that they say? 'What doesn't kill us makes us stronger?'"

"I think that's bullshit. It's a lie we tell ourselves to feel better."

"Yeah," he said. "Probably. But still, bad things happen, and though they may not make you stronger, if you're smart, they can make you money."

Then Feldman asked if I cried at Gene's funeral.

"Of course," I said.

"And now? Knowing everything you that you do, everything that he did, could you cry for him now?"

I thought about it. I admitted that though I had cried for Gene since I learned what he'd done, it had been different. It wasn't grief exactly, but something else.

Then Feldman smiled and asked if I was looking for work.

Our DistaGrieve service is Feldman's latest innovation. For an extra ninety-five dollars we'll record the ceremony, and then burn the footage to a DVD for family members that want to attend, but don't have the time or the money.

But today that seems to mean everyone. The entire family. Feldman and I are the only ones here. There's the deceased of course, and Father Bryan from St. Luke's, but he doesn't count. He's essentially a professional just like us.

Feldman hands me a video camera. "Keep your shots tight," he says. "Zoom in a lot. Let's not advertise the fact that there's not too many people here."

"There's no one here," I say, but Feldman waves this off. He tells me to get some footage of the tombstone.

So, I get some footage of the tombstone.

It reads: *Gone but not forgotten.*

I get some more shots of questionable usefulness: the leaden sky, the treetops swaying in the breeze, two squirrels fighting over an empty Doritos bag.

Then Feldman says it's time to begin the service. He positions one camera on a tripod in front of Father Bryan and the casket. The other he handholds a few feet from me.

"Okay," he whispers, "go ahead. Mourn."

I go through my routine. I think about how it felt to lose something only to learn none of it was real. I think about the times I catch Connie staring at me, and the way she smiles, and how I know it's love but feels more like pity. I think about the future.

But it doesn't work. Nothing happens. I scrunch my eyes tight, try to squeeze the tears out, but nothing comes.

"What's the problem?" Feldman says.

I shake my head.

"What is that? What does that mean?"

"I don't know," I say. "I can't do it. I can't cry."

"Jesus Christ," Feldman yells.

Father Bryan clears his throat, checks his watch.

"I don't need this right now," Feldman says. "Just try harder. You can do it. You're better than this."

But I'm not sure I am.

"Why didn't I ever have to take the Fish Test?" I say.

"What?"

"I'm the only one, right? So why me? Why didn't I have to take it?"

"I don't know. You didn't need it."

"What? What does that mean?"

Feldman sighs and stares at the ground, scanning it from left to right as if the answer is etched into the dirt and he is unable to find it. The camera, though still pointed at me, begins to droop in his hands. "Do you remember the night I offered you a job?" he says. "I asked if you had cried for your husband after everything that had happened?"

"Yes. So?"

"And you told me that you had. In spite of what he did, in spite of what you thought you knew about him, about your marriage, you still cried. Don't you get it? You've been crying for strangers since the beginning."

He's right. He's right and the truth of it hits me like something physical, something real. Like something I haven't felt in a long time. And even though it's the saddest, most pathetic-sounding thing I've ever heard, and even though the cameras are rolling, and Feldman and Father Bryan are staring at me, I can't help but laugh.

And laugh.

And laugh.

About the author:

Joe Dornich is a PhD candidate in Texas Tech's creative writing program where he also serves as Managing Editor for *Iron Horse Literary Review*. Joe's stories have won contests with *SCMLA*, *Fresher Writing*, *Master's Review*, and *Carve*.

OH, BROTHER!
©2017 by Ronna L. Edelstein

Vera sits on the floor, surrounded by a dozen photo albums, all different sizes and colors. She feels like the hub of a wheel with spokes of memories extending from her and toward her; she feels like Jupiter imagining its moons orbiting in a circular motion, never intersecting with one another.

Vera picks up the newest album—a bright red one she naively hopes will be filled with pictures of joy and optimism; it is only half-full so it feels light in her hands. She starts at the back, looking from right to left as if she were reading a text from her days as a Hebrew School student. Maybe by beginning at the end she can somehow manipulate time, can create a "back to the future" world in which Harry, her older brother by four years and only sibling, has not issued her a divorce decree with no possible chance of reconciliation. Perhaps she can change events so that now, at age forty-two, she does not have to face a future of being an only child.

This album, however, contains no pictures of Harry. Instead, Vera finds page after page of her now sixteen-year-old son and fourteen-year-old daughter: he playing basketball, she performing in school productions; he with his best friends at a pool party, she dressed to the nines for a father/daughter dance that she went to with the man next door. The camera has caught her children in smiles that do not quite hide the anger they feel at Vera for divorcing their father, at their father for separating himself from them, and at each other for just existing. The most special photos are the ones from Vera's parents' fiftieth anniversary dinner held only seven days ago. Vera had taken those photos of grandparents and grandchildren before the eruption—before Harry had grabbed his wife and stormed out of the restaurant, leaving behind the pieces of a sister he had chosen to shatter.

Harry had not always been a destroyer. Vera knows that her mind is not teasing her into believing that she and Harry had enjoyed good times together because photos in the oldest album, the ivory one with a rose on the front, confirm her memories. She flips through this album, being careful not to disengage the pictures from the four black triangles that hold them in place. Dad took these early photos with his Brownie camera; they are in black-and-white, a symbol, Vera thinks, of the simpler relationship she and Harry had. One photo captures the brother and sister, both dressed in overalls and snowsuits, building snowmen and white castles on the front lawn. Vera closes her eyes and hears Harry assuring her that he is her prince—the person who will always save her from witches who cackle and from queens who poison apples. In another photo, the snow has melted, and Vera and Harry each ride an ornate horse of the carousel at the local amusement park. They had galloped round and round, both trying to reach the magic ring. When the ride ended, Prince Harry had held out his hand and helped Princess Vera off her horse. A third photo captures two heads bobbing above the waves of the Atlantic Ocean. Later that night, she and Harry had stood side-by-side and oohed and aahed at the fireworks releasing an explosion of colors into the sky. Vera smiles at a picture of Harry curled up on his chair and Vera stretched out on the couch; both hold on their laps king-sized bowls of chocolate, vanilla, and strawberry ice cream topped with whipped cream, chocolate sauce, and a cherry. This is her favorite picture because ice cream before bed was part of the goodnight ritual she and Harry enjoyed—part of a time when war was a game of cards, not a state between two siblings.

In one photo, Harry stares solemnly at the camera, while Vera grins, revealing her lack of two front teeth. That picture had been taken on Valentine's Day when Harry, his rubber boots pounding against the snowy, icy sidewalk, had raced home halfway to school to retrieve the bag of valentines Vera had left on the kitchen table. Because of him, she was able to share cards with her first grade classmates.

The pictures in other albums are ones of color, giving Vera the red eyes that she always has before a camera and emphasizing Harry's chocolate brown eyes, dark hair, and good looks. Toward the back of one album, a black one with a hint of gray, Vera finds a photo of herself and Harry standing in front of the summer camp where she worked before entering college. Harry had driven several hours to see her; he had bought her a steak dinner at a nearby restaurant, but anything, even specks of tuna dripping under a sea of mayonnaise, would have tasted special to Vera because it came from Harry.

Yet, if Vera were honest with herself, she would admit that the albums capture only the positive moments. Neither she nor her parents had chosen to photograph a scowling Harry, a Harry with eyes raging with anger and with hands tightly clasped by his side— a Harry capable of the fury with which he erupted at the anniversary dinner.

There is no photo of the toddler who first looked at his newborn sister and cried,

"Monkey! Don't like it!" This story had become a family legend; it was told to relatives and friends, at holiday celebrations and during summer barbecues. Vera always laughed with the others. "Silly Harry," people would say fondly to the child, boy, teenager who had uttered these four words. Only Vera, as she got older and more perceptive, could recognize the hostility behind the words.

Harry had used the impersonal "it" to describe her; decades later, Dr. Harry, a physician with a busy practice, again demoted Vera to a thing, an object. "File her under 'F' for Fruit," he instructed his staff. Vera's teaching degree meant nothing to Harry; in his eyes, his sister was an emotional female who deserved little respect.

Although Harry never again called her a monkey, he had made it clear that Vera's appearance embarrassed him. "You will never win a beauty contest," he assured her. He took great delight in gloating that he had perfect teeth, pointing out that not even two years of wearing braces had straightened Vera's teeth. Harry used Vera's crooked teeth, overly large bottom lip, and chinless profile to paint a demonic picture that justified his dismissal of her—and his growing unwillingness to stand next to her in any photo-taking session.

But he had not stopped talking to her—or at her—until their parents' fiftieth anniversary celebration.

Although Vera wanted to play an active role in planning the golden anniversary dinner for their parents, Harry had made the decisions and then let Vera know the place and time. Determined not to let ill feelings ruin this special event, Vera and her two children had accepted Harry's coup of the occasion but had also worked hard to add their own touch to the celebration. Vera's son had created a song on his portable keyboard in honor of his grandparents, her daughter had written a lovely poem, and Vera had spent months putting together a pictorial/poetic album of her parents' lives. All three had looked forward to presenting their gifts at the anniversary dinner.

Prior to the dinner, Vera and her children had gone to Harry's office for optical exams. Just as they had chosen their new frames and were about to leave, Harry ordered Vera to follow him to his private office. As she meekly obeyed, she felt like the unruly child being summoned by the principal. Even before she crossed the threshold, Harry had barked, "Neither you nor your kids will do anything tonight to embarrass me! There will be no presentations or homemade gifts. If you disobey, I will leave." Harry pounded his fist on the desk—an exclamation point to his tirade.

Although Vera shook with fear, she mustered her courage to ask Harry why. "Because I said so!" he bellowed before storming out of his office. Like the cowardly lion in The Wizard of Oz, Vera gave in to his demand without a fight. She always gave in to Harry because Vera, the eternal cockeyed optimist, would do just about anything to avoid a confrontation.

When Vera shared Harry's decree with her children, however, they protested. Vera listened as her son and daughter, who had steadily been losing their closeness due to the hormones of the teenage years, spoke as one against Uncle Harry. "We worked hard to make Grandma and Grandpa's evening a special one," they argued. "Uncle Harry does not have the right to tell us what to do."

Vera pondered the situation as she and her children prepared for the evening. As she showered, she remembered when she and Harry had still been young enough to share a room. Vera had lain in her twin bed, separated from Harry only by a single nightstand. She had always wanted to reach her hand across that nightstand to hold onto Harry's hand for protection from the monster that she knew lived in the closet, yet she feared that Harry's reaction to her touch might be more venomous than anything the monster could do. Even at a young age, Harry could spit out words as if they were bullets shooting from a rifle.

When her family moved to the larger house with the extra bedroom, Harry had stared at Vera with eyes filled with hatred before going into the smallest bedroom, which he scornfully labeled "the cage." Vera had yearned to tell Harry that she envied him his privacy and that she worried about sharing a room, even one as large as the master bedroom, with Grandma, but six-year-old Vera understood that her ten-year-old brother too often used words as weapons to belittle and destroy, not to communicate.

Her children knocked on her bedroom door. "What did you decide to do, Ma?" they asked. Her son stared at her with unblinking eyes, while her daughter blinked back tears. "We're going with Plan A," Vera announced. "We will honor Grandma and Grandpa, and Uncle Harry will just have to grin and bear it."

Uncle Harry neither grinned nor bore. Between the appetizers and before the entrée, Vera's children had stood up, cleared their throats, and told their beloved grandparents they had prepared a special tribute for them. Grandma and Grandpa smiled, not seeing how Harry's face turned red with wrath. Before one song could be sung or one poem could be read, Harry slammed his fist on the table, causing the plates, glasses, and silverware to shake in fear, glared at Vera, and snarled, "You and I are through. We will never speak or see each other again." He then grabbed his wife's arm and left. Fortunately, their table was a corner one in an alcove so few other diners noticed the drama.

Five people—Vera, her two children, and her parents—finished the dinner like a Stepford family: they went through the motions, but they showed no emotion.

Now, a week later, Vera lies on her bed and contemplates Harry and his actions. Why does he only support and tolerate her when she follows his mandate? Why did her acting independently cause him to spit noxious words at her and then sever their sibling bond? Does he carry within a bad seed—something genetic that makes him act in such a dictatorial way? Or is he simply a bully who can only suppress his own insecurity by overpowering others? The complexity of her brother overwhelms Vera; she hugs her pillow for comfort.

Then, a memory slowly forms a picture in her mind. Vera searches through several more albums until she finds the photo she wants. It had been a hot April day in 1968. The family had gathered on the lawn of the local university to take pictures of Harry, a new graduate of the Medical School, and of Vera, a new graduate of the College of Arts and Sciences. Before the picture in the album of Harry and Vera holding their diplomas was taken, however, Harry had reached into a bag and removed four beautiful corsages; he handed a different one to each female member of the family. Each corsage came with a note in his handwriting: from your grandson, the doctor; from your son, the doctor; from your husband, the doctor; from your brother, the doctor.

From that moment on—from the second he hung a stethoscope around his neck and donned a white jacket—he was the doctor. He saw himself as smarter than Dad, an optometrist without a medical degree; as smarter than Ma, a woman whose immigrant family deprived her of a college education; and as smarter than Vera, a sister who dealt with literature and writing, not healthcare issues related to the field of ophthalmology. He adopted an officious tone; his communications consisted of his talking and then, depending upon the situation, either walking away or hanging up the phone. Maybe that medical degree gave him a much-needed identity; maybe he felt safer and stronger replacing his personality with that of the omniscient, omnipotent, god-like physician.

Vera sighs as she closes the album and places it next to the others on her bed. She then reaches to her headboard to turn off the light from the lamp Harry had carved to fulfill his junior high woodshop project. After he had earned his "A," Harry had dumped the lamp into the garbage, but Vera had furtively retrieved it. Harry, who refused to enter the master bedroom, especially after Grandma's move left the entire room to only Vera, never saw the lamp with the bamboo shade Vera had asked Ma to buy. The lamp has traveled with Vera to college and to graduate school, to the marital home and to the townhouse of divorce. Its glow has nightly illuminated the pages of Vera's before-bed book.

Before turning the switch, Vera stares at the light emanating from the lamp. It gives her a flicker of hope that maybe, some day, Harry will rescind his divorce decree, embrace her in a brotherly hug, and become a loving, supportive big brother—Wally Cleaver or David Nelson or any of those boys of the 1950s television shows that Vera had loved.

Yet, as she lies in her dark bedroom, Vera feels a profound sense of sadness and loneliness. She is convinced that Harry has forever banished her from his life. She believes without an iota of doubt that the "good" Harry—the one capable of kindness—no longer exists when it comes to her. No matter what roads she travels or what challenges she encounters, she will do so alone—as a younger sister who is an only child.

About the author:

As a part-time faculty member of the University of Pittsburgh's English Department, Ronna L. Edelstein works as a consultant at the school's Writing Center. She also teaches Freshman Programs, a course that introduces students to the University and the city. Her work, both fiction and nonfiction, has appeared in the following: "New Slang" A New Literary Voice by the Women and Girls of Pittsburgh" (online); *Quality Women's Fiction*; *Ghoti Online Literary Magazine*; *First Line Anthology*; *SLAB: Sound and Literary Artbook*; *Pulse: Voices from the Heart of Medicine* (online and print); *AARP Bulletin* (online and print); *Healthy Roots* (Forbes Health Foundation and Hospice); *The Jet Fuel Review* (Lewis University's online literary journal); Writer's Relief (online); *Seasons of Caring*; *Tales of Our Lives: Fork in the Road* (online e-book); *Signature* (Carnegie Mellon University Osher publication); *Verse Envisioned: the Poetry and Art of Pittsburgh*; *the Washington Post*; and the *Pittsburgh Post-Gazette*. "Oh, Brother!" is Ms. Edelstein's ninth Vera story to be honored by Scribes Valley Publishing.

JOHNNY FORWARD SOMEHOW KNOWS
©2017 by Hugh Dudley

My name is Jonathan Forward. I remember my dreams. Upon waking, I remember them, each one, very well. The dreams sometimes blur as my day progresses, but I remember all the essential points. I have been telling family members, schoolmates, college chums, and co-workers my dreams for years. My co-workers thought it was quite a gag when, for my fortieth birthday, they gave me a hardback copy of Freud's *The Interpretation of Dreams*. No one truly thinks that I am crazy; they chalk up my stories as eccentricity.

It started when I was five years old. I was just falling asleep when the train that runs through my hometown blew its whistle.

The train whistled. It scared me. I tried to yell out to warn my family. I called out. I wanted to be heard, but no sound would come out of my mouth. The train was getting closer and closer, becoming more and more dangerous. I had to take action or everyone would be injured. I leapt up standing in the middle of my bed. The train was on its tracks skimming the edges of the bed. The train followed the course, going round and round. I reached out to grab the train to make it stop, but there was nothing to grab hold of. The train kept moving, following the tracks at the edges of my bed. I yelled to warn my family.

When I woke up, my mother, father, and older brother were staring at me from the doorway of my room. They assured me that it was just a dream. And what's weird, I didn't understand what "just" meant in that context.

My name is Jonathan Forward. As long as I live, I will always remember a dream involving snakes.

My older sister and my Aunt Carol were walking ahead of my younger brother and me. We were walking in Austin Park. It's a pleasant, open park with no hint of danger. That's when I fell in the hole. It was a big hole. My brother fell in, too. There were snakes, lots of snakes. The snakes were attacking. I called out to my sister. I called out to my aunt. They were too far away. They couldn't hear me. I tried to protect my brother, but it was too late.

And then I woke up. There were no adults around on that occasion to console me. I just lay there, remembering and thinking about the dream. Why did I have the dream? I had never fallen into a hole before. I had never been abandoned by family members. Where had the images come from? And what's weird, I have never been afraid of snakes.

My name is Jonathan Forward. I am forty-five years old, have a great job as a bank teller, and am basically a happy person. I don't have a girlfriend right now, but my life is good without one. I am waiting for Miss Perfect to come along and take the name Mrs. Forward. The only disharmonious note in my life is that I remember my dreams.

I watch a science fiction show on NetFlix called *Star Travelers*. I know the episodes inside and out. I attend Travelers' Trivia nights and know all the answers. I can quote all the lines from Captain Smart and her crew as they travel their benevolent way across the galaxy fighting evil everywhere they encounter it. One morning, I woke from a dream.

I watched the opening credits of a Star Travelers *episode. Then the plot developed and the characters did what they do. Captain Smart, her starship, and the whole galaxy were put in jeopardy. I wasn't just a bystander. I was a member of the crew with a bit part. There was intrigue and a paradox to solve. The crew members did their jobs and the galaxy was saved. I watched the closing credits and listened to the ending theme music.*

A year or so later, at a Travelers Trivia party, I found myself in a fierce argument with Jimmy Rockland about a particular episode. Jimmy was a big-mouth and never knew as much as he thought he did. When the judge for the night asked which episode I was referring to, I told him. The whole group looked at me very strangely. I gradually realized, embarrassed, that the episode I was describing had actually been the episode I had dreamt. I had to admit my error to my friends and Jimmy. And what's weird, Jimmy Rockland never came back for trivia night after that.

My name is Jonathan Forward. My dreams seem so real to me, more so than what others say about their dreams. Perhaps because they are so vivid I remember them in detail. I am always me. My senses are alive. I see the entire spectra of colors, smells, and emotions. I respond to what is happening in all kinds of situations, including erotic encounters.

I stand at the bedroom door. Her hair, flowing over her shoulders, appears more chestnut brown with the light behind her. Watching as she works to open one bronze rivet button and then another on her denim jacket, I quietly and slowly raise the overhead light just enough to illuminate the side facing me well enough to enjoy her beauty. Her head finally shows the streaks of auburn gold I adore. The last button is undone and she relieves her splendidly firm shoulders of the heavy, blue cloth. Before me stands my goddess in a white veil of a blouse barely obscuring her beautiful, full breasts, as well as indigo-blue jeans clinging to her rounded hips. Light amber leather western-style boots with thick, tall heels adorn her feet. Her exceptionally balanced face is perfected by thin, wire-framed eye glasses.

She begins to undo the few buttons holding the blouse together. Her knees bend. She sits elegantly, almost floating, on the bed's edge just as her fingers find that last fastening. I move toward her just as she releases the button. My approach puts us knee to knee. She leans back just enough for me to gaze down at all of her incredible features. My own knees bend. I kiss her chin and move slowly down the centerline of her chest until my face rests contentedly in heaven.

The lady in my dream never has a name and always has the same auburn hair, voluptuous body, and perfect features. Yes, if I had to give her a name it would be Perfect. And what's weird, I'm not into big breasts.

My name is Jonathan Forward. I remember my dreams consistently, but I now suspect this is a character defect. Dreaming is a necessary part of sleep, but my dreams seem to be less and less beneficial to me as the years go by. Recurring dreams are a particular problem. Once a month or every other month I dream I can't remember where I left my car, finally finding the location only to find my car has been towed by an unscrupulous traffic warden. I always have a second car that I can drive. After all these years, I must have more than two hundred cars sitting in the local impound lot. And what's weird, no two are alike and not one of the cars is blue.

Many times, I have been in a town about to be hit by a tornado. The warning sirens blare. Everyone dashes for cover. I always see the twister as it passes, wreaking havoc. A few times, I have had the opportunity to walk right up to the churning cyclone to place my hand inside the column. I feel the wind swirling but I am never injured. And I never think it's weird I am always in the same town but never in the same location.

My name is Jonathan Forward. I have an excellent memory for all of the places I have been in my life, probably because I haven't been to too many. I have taken a few vacations to Hawaii and have traveled at Christmastime to New York City every third year since I was twenty-six. I remember the town I grew up in and the city I moved to as a young adult. I could close my eyes in any of those four places and still find my way around. My dreams take place in specific places. And what's weird, I have never been to any of the four places I have lived in my dreams.

Gunfire erupts in the distance. My companion and I are on the top floor of an apartment building. We hear a bang from the floor below. Our only escape is through the window. It is a five-story drop. We turn the dangerous corner to be out of sight of the window, hanging on the stone surface like a frog on terrarium glass. Our escape complete, we talk about what we want for dinner.

I have never been in that city yet it is home. All of my dreams are like that. It's always a place I know as well as any in my waking hours. It's always a place that is home. I never question my presence in a location during a dream. I have never seen them in films or photographs or on television. If they were at all familiar, I would not make a big deal of it. Dreams are a manifestation of current or past events in one's life. We simply do not make stuff up; we reorganize what we know. And I never think it's weird that I always speak the language and I can drink the tap water.

My name is Jonathan Forward. Now retired, I have been developing exercises of the mind to help me gain control of my dreams. Right before I go to sleep, I flush my mind of all that is real, closing my eyes and welcoming the black darkness and repeating over and over again, "I am in control." When I appear on the opposite side, I continue the exercise. I know control is the key. Upon awakening, I write down the events of my dreams.

I have learned much. There are two sets of worlds that I enter. When I have mental control, and enter a dream that contains nothing equal to the real world, I immediately awaken. I am getting close to proving we enter other real worlds when we dream.

I know I am not a neurologist or physicist. To prove my theory, I will need to explain it in professional terms. I have read books and articles and watched a lot of programs about the brain. If string theory is ever proven, we will be able to confirm that our universe is just one of many. Some scientists propose that we can enter these other universes by entering black holes. Others declare that if a rigid, enclosed surface is dynamically divided by zero, we could pop into an alternate universe. There are those who believe that when we die, we are reborn in another universe. The premise of my theory, in a nutshell, is: when we dream, we enter these alternate universes. My idea isn't so crazy and seems just as far-fetched as these others. I must prove it somehow before this gets too weird.

My name is Jonathan Forward. Tonight is the big night. I have practiced and practiced. I am going to find out what dreaming is all about. I am going to prove that we enter alternate universes when we dream. I'm falling asleep now...

I blink my eyes adjusting to the light. I am in a place, a field of sorts, grass and hills, and in the far-off distance I see buildings.

I am at the top of a hill looking out at the city, a city I don't recognize. Can I remember its name? Yes! It's Darrin City. There is no Darrin City that I have heard of, but I know my home is there. I am now walking toward the city. My steps are quick. I feel lighter than normal, almost as if I could jump and my feet would leave the ground and I would fly. This is a bit frightening, so I curl my toes in an effort to grab the grass below me to stay on the ground. I see two birds heading toward me.

Wait, they aren't birds! They're people! Flying people! I watch as they land about one hundred meters away. They walk toward me. And now, in this dream, yet reality, I walk toward them knowing that answers await my many questions.

It's a man and a woman. The man is my height and the woman has flowing brown hair streaked with gold. Her features are incredibly beautiful. As she comes closer, I notice her lovely, large breasts. She must have seen me leering; she takes a step back and hides behind her companion.

"Who is that man, Johnny? Why did we have to come and see him?"

The man motions the woman to stay behind and approaches

me. As he gets within a meter of me, he asks, "What are you doing here?"

I recognize his voice, but I wasn't sure where I had heard it before. I replied, "I have come to find out where I go in my dreams."

"You shouldn't have come here."

From behind, the girl yells out, "Johnny, be careful. He might hurt you!"

"He won't hurt me, dear. He can't. While he doesn't yet understand who he is, I know that he has no malicious intentions."

I don't understand why he is saying these things about me or why the woman is so frightened. I tell him, "I am only here to look for answers."

He asks, "What is your name?"

"My name is Jonathan Forward. I have come looking for the answers in my dreams."

My response is met with laughter. His face becomes recognizable. I know this man. I know his face. It's the same face I see in the mirror. How can this—

"You should not have come here, Jonathan. You broke the rules. There can only be one of us in this universe. My name is Johnny Forward. I am the one who is real here."

As the sense of recognition comes fully forward and the biting truth hits me, I wish for this dream to end.

I hear the man. "Wake up, Jonathan. Wake up now!"

With a phtzz and a poof I disappear.

My name is Johnny Forward. I had an odd dream last night. I'm used to having strange dreams, but this one takes the cake. I don't really remember that much of it, just the last bit. An entire universe popped out of existence. Completely. And what's weird, somehow I know it was my fault.

About the author:

Hugh Dudley is the pen name of Ken Dudley and his spouse, Bear Kosik. Ken is an information systems specialist with the State of New York. Bear is a full-time writer working in almost all formats.

THE FUTURE IS OURS
©2017 by Jean Tschohl Quinn

4:23 pm, Thursday October 5, 2000

Nura Zamani ran alone along the path. The rest of the cross-country team was ahead, far ahead, but she didn't care. It was her last practice. Sure, she'd run at the meet on Saturday, but that would be it. College aps were in, so she didn't need to anymore. Her heartbeat thumped against her ribcage. No more cross country. No more debate team. No more piano lessons. No more. No more. No more. She hit her goals. It would be an Ivy League because she deserved the best. Isn't that what she had been told all her life? Once she was in, she could do what she wanted...which was nothing. Her thick ponytail bobbed.

A fat woman in a jogging suit ran out from a bush and joined her. "Nura," she gasped, "can we talk?"

Nura shrugged, "Yeah, sure. Whatever." She jogged in place, "What do you want?"

The women exhaled heavily with her hands on her knees. "I'm your dire warning."

Nura stopped, resting her fists on her curvy hips, "Who are you?"

"I've come to warn you. If you don't change your attitude, you're going to end up like me."

"I don't even know you."

"Yes, you do. I'm you from twenty years in the future." She

straightened up and splayed her hands out, "This is what you'll look like by the time you're thirty-seven, if you keep up this attitude. You'll be fat and alone and poor."

Nura leaned back on one leg and crossed her arms, surveying the dark-eyed lump before her, "From the future?" The woman pulled a tarnished locket from inside her sweatshirt. She opened it to show a picture of Nura as a baby in the arms of her grandmother. Nura touched the one around her own neck with her right hand. With a tentative left index finger, she reached for the one resting in the palm of the older woman. They both jumped with a crackle of electricity. Nura rasped, "OK, sure. Why? What happens?"

The woman took the same stance, "Well, you go off to college, party, flunk out, have a series of dead-end jobs. Time passes and voila!" The woman shifts her weight to the other foot, "Change your ways and you'll have a chance."

Nura peered up into the oaks surrounding them, "And if I change my ways, how will you exist to tell me." She shifted her weight too.

The woman scowled, "They tell me you'll have a vague memory of this time. Look. This dimensional shift doesn't last long and a person can only do it once, so just change your attitude! You owe at least that much to your parents."

"I don't want to. That's all I ever do."

"Then, here's what you get." The woman smoothed the too tight jogging suit along the multiple bulges, "Is this good enough for you? Because it sucks for me."

"You're a nut job." Nura turned, jogging away from the woman.

"Yeah, sure. Whatever," she shouted after Nura.

3:43 pm, Sunday October 8, 2000

Claudette Ainsley Winslow's head rested on a vinyl cushion purloined from the garage. She lay on her back with one knee bent over the other, swinging erratically. It stopped mid-swing. She turned the last pages of the latest M. K. Bohnhoff science fiction epic with her eyes wide and the foot suspended by an invisible hook. She closed the book, slowly pulled her legs up to her chest, cradling the precious book to her chest, and sighed. She had escaped from her own twelfth birthday party and was hidden in her next-door neighbor's treehouse. She spent a lot of time there. Mrs. Jackson didn't mind; her kids were grown and gone. In fact, Mrs. Jackson was happy to see it still in use.

Voices floated up and over the fence from the party, breaking Claudette's reverie of Bohnhoff's time-travelers. "Has anyone seen Claudette? It's almost time for the cake!"

She sat up and peeped over the dry-rotted window sill. She knew she wasn't really missed. The guests were her parents' friends with their children. Any reason for a party was a good one, her mother always said. Her mother liked big things like parties and houses, and huge names for skinny, shy girls with lank brown hair and brown eyes. She wouldn't have hidden if she could have had a couple of her own friends. Just one would have helped. Just Derrick. Claudette knew better than to have expected her parents to invite him.

Derrick and Claudette had been friends since they met in kindergarten. He was gangly and skinny even then. His ears stuck out and his hair was nappy he said. He was the only black kid in their grade school. Claudette was not brave enough to stand up for him when he was teased during recess, but enough to sit with him at lunch. By second grade, Derrick's protruding ears, supported glasses. Claudette and he discussed books most kids their age wouldn't have touched and played in the safe neutrality of Mrs. Jackson's treehouse. He was going to love the time-travel story.

Now that she had finished the book, she was ready to return to the party.

A young woman, who looked vaguely familiar, beckoned from the bottom of the tree, "Hi, Claudette? Mind if I come up?" She was tall, Claudette could tell even from her vantage point on high. Her hair hung past her shoulders, brown with blue and green strands.

Claudette tried to be nonchalant, "Sure."

The woman ascended the two-by-fours nailed into the trunk with rusty familiarity. "I don't have long. Neither do you, I'd guess. Can we talk?"

Claudette was standing, backed into the corner, "Okay."

The young woman sat down on the cushion, "How do I say this?" She motioned to Claudette to join her. "Look. I'm you from the future, just like the book you're reading. Have you finished it yet? I loved that book." She shook her head and rolled her eyes, "Anyway, twenty years in the future." Claudette sat down next to the woman. "I don't think I can explain the technology in terms you can understand, but I wanted to talk to my younger self, so here I am."

Claudette looked at the book lying on the dusty floor of the treehouse and back at the woman. She blinked.

"I knew it could happen because I can remember this day, and this visit only...from your perspective." She looked around the treehouse wistfully, "First off, you will grow into your name. Think big, because you are big."

Claudette blinked again and stammered, "No, I'm not."

"I'm here to tell you, you are. I am. *We* are! Look. It will take some courage and your parents are really smart. You can trust them. They will give you the best advice. Then, get back to the party and have confidence!" She jumped up and took the two steps to the propped-up hatch.

"What's the scar on the back of your calf?"

The woman stopped and felt the long-healed, still-angry red line on the back of her right calf, trailing downward from under her capris, "Oh, that." She weighed her words, "Rolling down the hill on a midnight picnic your junior year of high school."

"But what if I don't?"

She paused and smiled. "I don't know. I gotta go." She descended a few of the two-by-fours, when she looked back at little Claudette. "Oh, and be wary of anything to do with Derrick." She continued her descent.

Claudette scrambled for the hatch to follow, glancing back at the book for a moment. "Why? Why Derrick? He's my best friend." She jumped down, skipping the last few makeshift rungs, and stumbled. Her older self was gone.

Saturday, 8:33, August 27, 2016

Nura Zamani-Rahbar, now thirty-three, threw her Ogio bag onto the backseat of her Lexus RC-350 and drove away from Flywheel Sports in a hurry. Instead of getting on the I-405, she pulled into the Hilton Bellevue. She parked with a screech and walked directly into *Basil's* for a drink or two. Why go home to the sterile house with the brooding husband before absolutely necessary?

In the Bellevue Hilton Ballroom, the head cheerleader of ten years earlier spoke from the podium, "...so let's raise a glass to Bellevue High School, Class of 2006!"

A 28-year-old woman, in a sea of 28-year-olds, with pink highlights in her mousy hair pushed her glasses up her nose, swallowed the last of her champagne and set the glass on the nearby table. She straightened her well-tailored evening suit and walked straight toward the exit. A black man with a powerful build watched her walk by, pushed his glasses up his nose, gave a quick nod to his companions and followed her out. "Claudette," he whispered. As his long strides closed the gap to her, his volume increased, "Claudette!" She turned to look at him. "Claudette Ainsley Winslow, it's me."

"Derrick?" she peered at him from the dimly light foyer. The glow from the banquet hall gave him a halo as he approached her. He picked her up and swung her around. She giggled.

Derrick scanned around her, looking for a date, perhaps. "It's so good to see you." They beamed at each other and fell into conversation like the two friends they had been in grade school. He grabbed her hand and towed her into the hotel bar. "In here. It'll be quieter." They snaked through the ferns and pools of light cascading from the shelves of liquor bottles to find a booth off to one side with mostly empty tables around them, save for a carefully-coifed, exotic-looking, dark-haired woman rubbing her forehead. Her other hand gently tapped the side of her empty highball glass with the dredges of something viscous and green in it.

They exchanged the requisite biographies of the ten years since high school graduation. Derrick had founded a small company that was about to be subsumed by Microsoft. He owned his own townhome in Redmond, nothing spectacular but it was his...and the bank's. Claudette was finishing up her PhD in Physics, sharing graduate housing near the UW labs. A comfortable silence passed between them for a full minute when Derrick sighed. "What happened to us?"

Claudette pushed her spine into the brocade of the cushioned seat, "What do you mean?"

"I mean, we were best friends all through grade school. Then, in middle school, you dropped me. Nothing. That was it."

Claudette blushed, "I can't tell you, really."

"Can't or won't?"

"I wanted to stay friends but..." She slumped. Another minute of silence passed, this time not so comfortably. She leaned forward, "I almost tried to talk to you about it after some football game our junior year. I was surprised to see you there. You weren't exactly a fan."

He leaned in and laughed, "*Shhhh*. You can't say you're not a football fan aloud in the state of Washington." Claudette laughed too. They locked eyes. Claudette broke contact and looked at his broad shoulders, then the ceiling. Derrick sighed, "I was a late bloomer."

"You were so skinny."

"Yes, the stereotypical non-threatening black man—skinny, glasses, backpack, and sensible shoes. Bless my mamma and her Northwest ways."

"You grew into your ears too." Claudette teared up, "I'm so

sorry." She put her hand on his. Their eyes locked again. She smiled, "The Clark Kent glasses are working or you'd be downright menacing now."

He bared his teeth in an over-sized smile and whipped off his glasses. They laughed. He squinted and put the glasses back on. "So, what happened on the night you were almost going to tell me?"

She gave a heavy sigh as she decided how to edit the story. "Some girls were having a sleepover, an excuse to sneak over to the park behind the school to party. I saw you sitting on a blanket on the top of the hill."

Derrick hung his head over his drink. "Oh. I remember that night. I *thought* I was meeting Allison Chow for a midnight picnic. She never showed. It was so humiliating."

Claudette squeezed his hand again, resting her chin on her other hand. "I started toward you but changed my mind and ran back to the others."

Derrick withdrew his hand. "Why did you change your mind?"

She, too, pulled back her hand, slid it down under the table and she felt the calf of her right leg. It was smooth. "You'll think I'm crazy."

He smacked both hands on the table. "Just tell me."

She stumbled over her own words. After several false starts, she blurted out, "I was visited by my future self when I was twelve years old and she told me to stay away from you!"

Derrick blinked. The woman at the table nearby whipped her head around. "What? What did you say?"

Derrick cocked his head towards her. "Excuse me? This is a private conversation."

It was too late. The woman tottered over to them and slid into the booth next to Claudette. "The same thing happened to me."

Claudette clutched the arm of the woman. Derrick stammered, "You were told to stay away from me too?"

Both women looked at Derrick. "No."

Nura and Claudette spoke in a flurry about what happened to

each of them. Derrick tried to follow, catching only some of Claudette's words.

"That's why I'm studying Physics—I know time-travel is possible because I've already met myself from the future. I know I'll be successful. That's why I can be so confident about my work. Tell me everything."

His mind reeled. By the time he tuned back in, the other woman was speaking.

"Then, about five minutes later, this amazing, beautiful woman—I mean me—ran up to me on the path and said, 'You did it! You changed your attitude. You'll have a wonderful life. Just keep achieving.' Then, I heard a siren and she was gone." Nura dropped her head forward, bouncing it off her fisted hands resting on the table in front of her. She sat up, "Look. Yes, I'm a PhD, married, and thin."

"And beautiful," Derrick interjected.

Nura paused for a moment, brushed his hand lightly with a perfectly manicured hand, and smirked. She continued, "And I am miserable. I hate my job. I hate my husband. I hate all the expectations. I hate the regimens. I hate it all. I hate it. I hate it. I hate it. It's not wonderful. It's terrible. I just don't get it."

Claudette bounced on the seat. "So that means the future isn't set!" She pulled out a tablet from her purse. "I've got to get this down." Tapping wildly on the screen, she spat out rapid-fire questions, "Can I record this conversation? Could repeat your story? Why can they only visit once? Why did I only meet me once? Explain the second visit again. And if your future self can change, the new one gets a turn too. How many alternatives are possible? Your memory doesn't seem vague, does it? Are you making different decisions than you would presumably? Are you sure you still won't get fat in time in the next four years? Did she mention remembering the fat-you meeting? 'Dimensional shift' you say? Did she say anything else about that? So why hasn't my future me returned with technical help? I didn't get the scar, so I changed *her* scar. So, it's a different future. Why didn't my scarless me visit? If it didn't matter, then why would I remember that part? It's kind of vague, or is it? What else did I change? Don't worry about that."

Derrick, forgotten, stared at them in the semi-darkness.

10 am, Thursday October 5, 2000

In addition to the tutoring and counselling services, and the huge commerce and merchandizing branding, Star Parenting Inc. offered options for truly desperate parents for the right price. Only the most affluent and concerned parents were invited to learn more. The authenticity or nobility of the concern was not evaluated.

A certain elevator at SPI Headquarters required a handprint scan. Russel Panthulu rode down, down, down, finally exiting that same elevator. He unlocked his office door, fussed with his jacket and briefcase, gazing intently at the master schedule displayed on a whiteboard as his day began. An ethnically ambiguous looking man knocked on the doorframe, "Russel, do you have a moment?"

Russel startled slightly as his concentration broke, "Oh, Thomas. Thank you for coming in. Have a seat." They both sat. Russel leaned his elbows on his desk, bridging his hands. "So, yesterday was your last day in the field. You've done a great job, nearly 200 cases in three years. Very high customer satisfaction ratings. We at SPI want you to know just how pleased we are with your work. Are you sure we can't talk you into staying on?"

Tom shook his head. "No. It's time for me to go. Is there something I need to sign?"

Russel laughed, "Of course there's something for you to sign! When you joined us, you signed a fully binding non-disclosure agreement and a promissory agreement that you would indeed abide by the post-employment, non-communication, non-disclosure, non-compete agreements." He pulled a file from his center drawer. "This is just a reiteration of those contracts. A reminder, if you will." He pushed the papers towards Tom.

Tom nodded and signed, only briefly glancing at the papers.

"You've done great work here. You've been a real asset to the company. It's not too late to change your mind."

With a thin smile, Tom pushed the papers back to Russel. "No, it's time for me to move on. I'd really like to pursue my original goals."

Russel slid another, smaller piece of paper towards him. Tom looked at it, a number. "What's this?"

"It's a severance gift. Rest assured," Russel stood, leaning forward on his desk, "there is no problem with you going. However, once you go, it's best that you just forget you ever worked here...and that we never will." He lifted his index finger to his smirking lips.

Tom stood, "Mum's the word." They shook hands.

Russel clapped his hands together. "Well, I must get back to work. Feel free to say your good-byes leisurely. It's a relatively quiet day. You can help in the workroom if you wish. I don't mind." He ushered Tom out of the office. "I trust you," he winked.

Together, they walked to a set of double doors. Together, they entered a large open room: part Salon, part Green Room.

Tom peeled off towards the costume closet into the arms of an elderly woman with a tape measure draped on her shoulder.

Russel approached a round woman contouring her face with a powder a few tones darker than her complexion. He quickly flipped through the dossier. "Carla, you have really captured the shape of her nose," he considered her face, "but that mole isn't quite right." He picked up the folder and held it out to her. "See, in this picture it's in line with the corner of her right eye." They looked at the photograph together. "Maybe it's clearer on another picture." He pulled out another clandestinely-taken picture.

"Ah, I see. Thanks, Rusty."

His eyes darted right and left at the nickname; his cheeks flushed. Recovering, he held up his hands in mock protest. "Hey, I'm only saying it to make myself sound useful. You are a master at this." She shifted the removable mole slightly. He called to a raven-haired beauty on the other side of the room. "Eva, come compare make-up, please."

After Carla applied a few swipes of concealer on Eva's collar bone to cover an actual mole and a shift of the removable one near Eva's right eye, Carla and Eva examined each other side by side in the mirror. All three gave thumbs up. Eva, curvaceous and dressed in tailored workout clothes, walked to wardrobe to say good-bye to Tom.

Carla slid a locket out of a plastic sleeve stapled to the dossier. Russel helped her fasten it around her neck. He fished a tiny wire from the back of her sweatshirt and twisted onto the necklace's clasp, "Give it a test." She pressed a button sewn into the ribbing at the bottom of the sweatshirt. A crackle of static hit them both. They giggled. Russel glanced around the room to note any observers. "I'm really sorry that you have to wear the yellow jogging suit. It's supposed to be too small...to show off your, um, curves. I hope that's okay."

Carla sighed. "I know, I know. It's another cautionary tale gig. It's my own fault for being...zaftig. Geez, you'd think these parents would care a little less about whether their daughters end up fat."

He smirked as his eyes trailed down her rolls. "Look, you want the paycheck or not?" he teased.

"Of course I want my paycheck. It's a good one," she smiled as he walked away. A hair assistant sauntered over, shaking a can of black hairspray while carrying a wig head which she set down at the next station. No one was at the station, but a satchel was perched on the swivel chair. Carla mumbled to no one in particular, "Even with the non-disclosure agreement."

A woman in her early thirties with short blondish hair followed closely behind the hair assistant and carefully examined the wig of thin mousy hair artfully highlighted with blue and green streaks. Out of the side of her mouth, she whispered back to Carla, "That's for sure. I don't know how I'll ever have a real career if I stay here much longer."

The assistant carefully sprayed Carla's chestnut hair with the temporary color, gathering her thick hair into a messy topknot.

Carla laughed ruefully and added, "What are you doing in today? I thought your 'performance' was on Saturday."

"I was studying the dossier and wanted to make the hair a little bolder. Thanks, Kelli. I think that will work just fine," she added in the direction of the hair assistant. "I want to get over to the neighbor's house while she's out, so I can practice climbing the treehouse like I'm remembering it. I'm still a method actor, after all."

About the author:

Jean Tschohl Quinn's Gramma Mayme told her to "bloom where you're planted" when she was little (Jean, not Mayme). As life has bounced her about, Jean has had to do just that. A few of her short stories and commentary have been published (*Under the Rose* by Norilana Press, Scribes Valley anthologies four years running, theflashfictionpress.org, and *This Is Terrible* by ADBooks). She, a mathematician by degree and musician by choice, is currently working on a MFA in Creative Writing from Antioch University in which she impetuously enrolled "for an external goal" after she and her husband became empty-nesters and moved to another state in the same week.